The Sleep Thief

The Sleep Thief

Ibtisam Azem

Translated from the Arabic
by Sinan Antoon

&

SHEFFIELD – LONDON – NEW YORK

First published in English in 2026 by And Other Stories
Sheffield – London – New York
www.andotherstories.org

9 8 7 6 5 4 3 2 1

ISBN: 9781916751538
eBook ISBN: 9781916751545

Editor: Tara Tobler; Copy-editor: Gesche Ipsen; Proofreader: Alex Middleton; Typesetter: Tetragon, London; Typefaces: Albertan Pro and Linotype Syntax (interior) and Stellage (cover); Series Cover Design: Elisa von Randow, Alles Blau Studio, Brazil, after a concept by And Other Stories.

And Other Stories books are printed and bound in the UK on FSC-certified paper by Short Run Press Ltd, Exeter.

A catalogue record for this book is available from the British Library.

And Other Stories' Authorised Representative within the EU GPSR legal framework is: Logos Europe, 9 rue Nicolas Poussin, 17000 La Rochelle, France. (Logos Europe do not represent to publishers the rights to this title.) Email: contact@logoseurope.eu

And Other Stories gratefully acknowledge that our work is supported using public funding by Arts Council England.

ARTS COUNCIL ENGLAND
Supported using public funding by
ARTS COUNCIL
ENGLAND

FSC
www.fsc.org
MIX
Paper | Supporting responsible forestry
FSC® C014540

CONTENTS

THE SLEEP THIEF

'Sleep thief' is what the interrogator called me. I'll never forget that. I would steal a few seconds of sleep so I could remain steadfast before them. The name stuck; I even dreamt about it, the same dream, night after night. I would wake up not knowing what to do and drenched in sweat.

I cried until my eyes became so puffy they outgrew my face and enveloped it entirely. At night the gods came down to comfort me and wipe away my tears. But nothing relieved me. I cried so much my eyelids swelled over my eyes. I could barely see. I asked the gods to give me back my yesterday; they refused, except for one, the kindest among them. Upon me he bestowed the gift of stealing sleep so I could dream. The dream, he said, was the seed of a long path still ahead.

Had the kind god not set conditions, he would not have been a god. He relayed the same message every night: 'You have had your usual third of sleep. You need a second third, however, to continue the dream of retrieving your yesterday, and in that you cannot sleep unless you take the life of another human. All you must do is find someone to stare into your eyes. When they do, you will have their life, and dream of whatever you desire, and you will inch closer to retrieving your yesterday.'

The gods depart before hearing me accept or decline. I do not like the gift. I do not wish to steal sleep from anyone. Nor do I want anyone's life. The one I have is enough. If I live and still have tears in my eyes, I will not die of thirst.

I forget the gods' gift and go out into the street. I see my family. They are all staring at me, happy to see me. I steal their lives, despite myself, and remember what I have become. I shut my eyes over what remains of the dream. I only open them again in a dark room, where no one can gaze into them.

Every night I spend the rest of the dream staring at the night's kohl.

The same dream recurs every night.

The dream recurs.

I am still a sleep thief. When will I have a different dream?

Gharib Haifawi
The Sleep Thief

GHARIB HAIFAWI

No one knows exactly who gave Gharib Haifawi his name, or why. Some say it was his mother, Alya Haifawi, because he was born in a strange time. There are those who claim she felt like a stranger in the village of Alaf in the Galilee. Alya had lived there after getting married and gave birth to Gharib, who was her firstborn, during the Six Day War. Perhaps she gave him his name because that war was so short and strange. Alya didn't live in Alaf for long and returned to Haifa; whoever lives on Mount Carmel must return or else they will die of sorrow.

It was not strange that war had roamed the country. That was perfectly normal. The war was merely resting. Even wars tire. But it *was* strange for a war to have been so short. It left just as people were getting used to it. Some malicious folk jibed that the people of Haifa and nearby villages came out with placards to protest the end of a war to which they'd become so happily accustomed.

What is important in our story is Gharib Haifawi himself. No matter the divergent opinions regarding his name's origin, what is certain and unequivocal is that 'Gharib', in Arabic, comes from the root 'gh.r.b'. The following terms are derived from it: estrangement, west, to set, strange, to find strange, stranger . . . and so on. There is such significance in the etymology of this name, no?

Gharib Haifawi was born on the 11th of May to Adil and Alya Haifawi. Their surname refers to those hailing from Haifa, and in common parlance has a geographic association, though it usually begins with the definite article 'al-'. One is called al-Haifawi: of Haifa. There are those who say that the name goes back to Gharib's maternal grandfather. Arabs, after all, took their mothers' names in olden times.

Gharib's grandfather was a merchant, like all his ancestors ever since the day the Greeks boarded their ships and docked at Haifa to fall in love with it, just as it fell in love with them. They only left to roam the sea and yearn for Haifa. What is also certain, based on sound evidence, is that Gharib's origins go back to Greek merchants and Canaanites. This is proven by archaeology, genealogy and other evidence found in our archive.

The word 'archive' had a strange resonance for Gharib, suggesting incontrovertible proof, truths that could neither be debunked nor falsified. He also had a soft spot for the university archive at which he worked. He spent long hours reading there and many fond memories were born in its darkness.

Gharib was obsessed with the names of objects and the meanings of words. After much searching in the archive for the possible meanings of the word Palestine, he chose a narrative redolent of sea waves. He would repeat PALESTINE to himself as if he were touching every letter with his tongue. Turning the letters in his mouth as if tasting a piece of dessert. He wanted to remind himself that even if they banned its use, he would not forget the country they executed. But it didn't die: it was resurrected.

He liked the narrative that attributed the name to seafarers from Greek islands who settled here. In that story, the place took their name. That story had the scent of the sea. When he was a teenager, he always told his friends: The Greeks love us so much! Whenever Greek teams played Maccabi Tel Aviv in the European Basketball Championship, he would say, look how they raise Palestinian flags. He used to cheer for any team that played against Maccabi. Their players were so arrogant, he would say. But he was bothered by more than that. What really drove him mad was the Israeli flag fluttering after they won. Gharib also detested the sight of people chewing gum with their mouths open; the tongue and teeth could be seen rumbling and moving as if in battle. Many basketball players used to do that, but Gharib only had eyes for the open mouths of Maccabi Tel Aviv.

His family called the year he was born 'the year of the Naksa'. 1967. Gharib could have resented being born in those circumstances and in that year. Instead, he consoled himself with an excess of optimism. 'That's alright,' he would say. 'If I first set eyes on this world in days of war, then surely whatever comes after must be better!' Too often, however, dark pessimism would follow. Our friend Gharib and his people oscillated between these extremes. As if this pessoptimism, as that famous writer with a raspy voice and piercing look once said, was unwilling to part company with them. It should come as no surprise that they are oscillating still. As their prophet predicted, they remain trapped in that spot.

Gharib's eyes were honey-coloured, neither big nor small. He had thick eyelashes, as if a painter had just finished drawing them in kohl. His curly hair was rings blending the colours of sun and earth. He was of medium height, despite his hope and constant attempts to grow taller by playing basketball. Eventually he was convinced that 'the middle is best', as an Arab proverb insists.

What follows, dear reader, is Gharib's story. Or to be more precise, the story of a few days in Gharib's journey. When it began he was still sauntering on Haifa's beach and toying with its sands, before a sinister wave came and stole the grains squatting on his feet. You can identify Gharib on Haifa's beach by the slight bend in his neck that he tries hard to get rid of, or, at times, hide.

Dear reader, since Gharib does not like others to speak for him, he has taken matters in hand and said a few things he wanted us to know about those days. All I have done is collect his words and put them in story form. I will not deny that I have used my authority as a narrator and interfered, here and there, in those matters that Gharib did not wish to, or could not, describe. But they are few and far between.

THE WINDS OF OCTOBER

My body rolled and my face wallowed in sand after they threw me out of the car onto the lips of Haifa's shore. Mount Carmel looked on. The sand paid no attention to me. It lay there, unperturbed. As usual at this time of year, the sea was in a capricious mood, the October winds declaring their might over it, by turns teasing and storming its waves.

Why did they choose this side of the shore to dump my body? Only a week ago, nearby, I had trembled as I touched and kissed Hamsa's breasts, every pore in them opening lazily to my skin, languid as almond blossoms in spring. Her lips were flush. The moon stayed up, hauling in its light and casting silver nets over her hair, her thin dark body, her full chest. Hamsa was undressing and touching my body as if seeding a pomegranate. Making sure to kiss and touch every single seed.

I had been busy protesting. Less than an hour ago, I was chanting and throwing rocks like everyone else, until they caught me. I was terrified.

'Come here, you son of a sharmuta,' said one of them between slaps. They dragged me by the neck so hard it nearly snapped. The car drove on with curses. Suddenly they pulled over at the beach, stopped slapping and threw me out. They bade farewell in a flood of spit. Why had they left the crowd downtown and brought me to the beach? Did they know I was here with Hamsa a week ago? I imagined they knew everything, without a doubt. It made no sense to lie to them. They had parked far away, but were watching my reaction.

They spat. They threw me out of the police car and spat at me. Their breath stank. Like I was a bin for anyone to toss their trash into. Afterwards I could not shower or splash water across my body without feeling them spit again. This lasted for years. I was forced to taste their spit because my mouth was open. The pain from their punches made me scream.

Where is she? She was with me just now. Before they pulled me by my long and curly hair from the crowd and stuffed me into the car and beat the shit out of me. Seconds before that I'd been holding her hand so she wouldn't get hurt. Did they drag her to one of those cars too? Did they call her names just as they did with me? Did they call her a whore? Did they grope her?

Night had put on its blackest kohl and the moon had been banished; only the god of eternal loneliness sat serenely on the sky's throne. I was cast on the shore under this sky. I felt the earth moving beneath me, but strangely, without shaking. The more I scrutinised the darkness the more its kohl intensified. There was no trace of the sea. I could hear its bluster but I saw nothing.

When the ants climbed all over me and touched me, it was then that I touched darkness. I was a corpse and couldn't move. But I wasn't afraid. The only parts of my body I could move were my pupils. They expanded to swallow the darkness. All of it.

Things spiralled out of my control that day. I felt like a boat whose captain has drowned, still sailing at the whim of the winds and waves.

'Gharib, habibi, let's go to the protest and show solidarity with the people in the West Bank. They have to know that we won't be silent about what they are going through. Our voices must be loud in this country. If they don't want to hear our voices, we must force them to listen no matter what,' Hamsa said confidently. I didn't like going to protests. With a tense smile on my lips, I whispered in her ear: 'I'll go just for you.'

These protests were later called the October Uprising. Thirteen people were killed in a few days. Yitsik, the grocer, who lived in our neighbourhood, was upset, compulsively voicing disappointment at 'Israeli Arabs', as he like to call Palestinians. 'It's like an intifada,' he said, the disapproval vivid on his face. 'As if we are in the territories. That can't be, Gharib! The Arabs cannot let us down this much. They are behaving like the people in the West Bank. How can we trust them?'

I was astonished that he was astonished and told him he should have joined us, so we could have fought together. He raised his eyebrows and severed that conversation just like limbs in war. We talked about the weather and then retreated into our shells. Soon after, when the second intifada eclipsed all other news, the rift between us became a black hole.

Some Palestinians inside were trying to repackage what the protesters did, couching it in phrases like 'immature behaviour' to wipe the sweat off the foreheads of their astonished Jewish neighbours and friends. Others, however, saw the rift growing, so they struck again to enlarge it still more. Because life had become so unbearable. As if they were saying: Listen to us or we will all end up dead together in this grave called Israel!

I had nothing to do with protests or demonstrations, despite my firm belief in people's right to protest their conditions, not to mention my belief in the importance of doing so. But something in them scared and suffocated me. I was forced to go because I had promised Hamsa. More importantly, I was afraid to let her to go alone. I clasped her hand. I don't know how they picked me out amid the chants, or how her hand slipped from mine.

Not a single body part gave in to motion. Only my eyes consented to my closing them after they swallowed all the darkness. I was afraid that I would go blind. My mother used to tell me that would happen if I kept staring at the sun. I thought staring into the darkness might do the same thing, so they shut.

Ants swarmed my body and covered it. Had it not been for my breath, in and out, under the ants, I would have thought that I was dead, an ant-covered pile of trash.

Tick tick tick tick. That's how I felt. They often spoke of Palestinians as a ticking demographic bomb. Arabs were ticking bombs inside the country. At times, I used to walk around and feel like I could explode at any minute.

Tick tick tick tick. My eyes were shut. I could hear the ticking all around. Tick tick tick tick tick tick tick tick tick.

Hamsa's warm voice made its way through to me; her body was leaning over mine. 'Gharib, get up. Let's go. It's a long way.' She wiped the ants off my body with confidence. I was surprised that she wasn't repulsed. We walked side by side.

She smiled as if God was manifested therein. I asked her:

'Where is he?'

'Who?'

'The One. Please tell me you know who I mean!'

'Don't you know that he abandoned us a long time ago? Are you one of the seven sleepers?'

THE SHIN BET HONOURS GHARIB WITH A VISIT

That last rock was an offering for Hamsa, but the preceding ones were for other things. Mainly a desire to cast away the fear I had within. The army and border guards terrified me. They were feared like gods in our neighbourhoods. We only saw them when there was a political crisis. Otherwise, our neighbourhoods were ours. I wanted to kill the fear I had of these gods within me.

I used to walk and turn suddenly, convinced I was being tracked. Even in the bathroom I felt watched. 'Devils and angels surround you, and each tries to conscript you to its ranks,' they used to tell us in school: 'God has eyes watching you everywhere. His angels record your deeds.'

When I was a teenager, I once fled the bathroom before I could even finish peeing. An entity stood in the corner, eavesdropping on my thoughts. My thoughts were glowing and shivering as they traced the breasts of a girl in my class. I pulled up my trousers quickly and went into the living room where my brother Na'im and my mother were sitting.

I remember one evening when the sky was cloaked in the colour of mourning. It seemed to me that the scent of death I so often smelt from all directions had now suffocated the city. My cousin Zakiyya died. Her smile had fled a month before. She returned from the hospital only to be put in a coffin that same day; when she left, she took the laughter from everyone's faces with her to the sky.

Zakiyya used to spend the day at my uncle's store, counting every second of those long hours. I'd make multiple trips to the store daily, picking up whatever my mother suddenly remembered she needed. Those constant trips drained me and it showed. Zakiyya's smile was always welcoming. She would caress my curly hair in consolation.

Her dying was my first taste of death. I had only smelt it before, when I was told about how my paternal grandfather died before I was born, or when I heard of someone dying in our neighbourhood. But none of them had caressed my hair like Zakiyya. I had repeatedly asked my mother about what happened to the dead after burial, prompting her to finally explain heaven, hell and the torment of the grave.

I think I was five. I extended my hands and looked at them, wondering what this life meant if it was going to end. This question never left; it only became more complicated.

I became obsessed and terrified by the torment of the grave, worrying that loved ones might not go to heaven, or that I might not either. I started feeling as if I was carrying the scales of deeds everywhere I went, weighing and then sweating out of fear.

It was a disaster when yet another eye started watching me: the eye of the state.

'They know everything about you, man. If they catch you, they'll fuck you over. No point hiding anything from them.' Husam used to parrot this line of his father's, and I wasn't much better. I, too, used to repeat and believe what my father said. Or I did until I couldn't take any more fear, and decided to slam the door shut in its face once and for all.

I was sixteen and, other than sleeping and eating, I had found new ways to pleasure myself. Masturbation became my favourite hobby. As much as I loved to watch TV, sleep, play sports or read, it was masturbating that became a kind of prayer. I couldn't imagine ever stopping. Local newspapers were full of ads for phone-sex lines, which boasted that they catered to every language in the country. I was stunned when I discovered that there were Arab girls working those lines. Husam, however, said they were probably Jews from Arab countries. 'No Arab girl is willing to do it. These are Jewish girls pretending to be Arab. They hire them specially to fuck up our society.' He said it again, and with such confidence you'd think he had seventy years' experience in sex work. I didn't give a damn about Husam's theories. All I cared about was jerking off to a balmy voice.

I remember that Saturday vividly. My family was out. Studying was an excuse to stay home. My mother usually forgets something and would come back to get it. After they left, I waited a quarter of an hour and then took the phone to my room. I closed the door and checked several times that it was locked. I took off my pants and called one of the lines and started to play with my penis. The voice on the other side was warm. I was going to burst at any moment, but I didn't want to come in less than a minute, so I rubbed more gently and said nothing. The woman with the warm voice said how much she craved me. Naively, I believed she was talking to me, me personally, even though she could only hear my scorched breathing. My body felt like a volcano, and I was about to come when I suddenly heard crackling. It shattered my lust and turned it cold. My blood had been racing and searching for a way out, but now it froze. Maybe it was just normal static? Nothing mattered at that moment. All I could imagine was the Shin Bet spying on Palestinian phonelines. I didn't consider the logistics, whether carrying such a thing out was even possible. The suspicion was there. That was sufficient to pull strings of horror.

I imagined one of them listening to the tape and calling his colleagues over. They would ridicule me and my heavy breathing. It could be someone I knew. I felt naked and skinned.

I stopped masturbating for a whole month and the phone was no longer of any use. I was saved only when Husam came over one evening to tell me that he and two others wanted to form a cell. We were to throw Molotov cocktails at the police station, print and distribute leaflets against oppression, and raise Palestinian flags on Land Day. I agreed because it seemed to be the only way to rid myself of this horror they planted inside me: the state.

We formed our cell, threw Molotov cocktails and printed the leaflets. But that type of work called for some sort of commitment. I discovered during the leaflet phase that I didn't like discipline or being boxed in with a group. Less than two months later I quit. Soon after, the others did too.

Conquering that first fear was important. Others followed. The Shin Bet and the army were no longer fearsome monsters or gods. I immersed myself in my studies and forgot all about the cell and its members, until one terrible evening when I was visited by a tough-looking man. The visit was a surprise; it came four years after I had thrown the last rock.

I was in my second year at the Hebrew University of Jerusalem. I had returned to my dorm, drained and drunk, barely able to keep the alcohol in my stomach. I don't know how I even found my way to my room and bed. Thank God my room-mate was not there.

The moment I drifted off to sleep I heard assertive knocks on the door. I was sure I opened my mouth and my tongue enquired who was there; no answer came. The hand was determined. I could not get rid of the knocking person. I had failed. So I got up and went to open the door.

'Good evening. Are you Gharib Haifawi?'

'Good morning is more like it. It's one a.m.!'

Although the ground was still drunk-dancing around me, I could recognise his serious looks and the matter of importance they denoted, so I remedied my response.

'Yes, I am Gharib Haifawi. What do you want?'

'Argos wants to see you in person. That's all we can say at this point.'

'Argos? Never heard of him.'

'That's all we can say. Put on your clothes and come with us right away!'

'So it's an order?'

'Yes, and it must be followed immediately.'

I put on a pair of jeans I'd recently bought and a white shirt, nabbed at a glance from the pile of clothes by my bed. I went out with the man and was soon stormed by confusion; a huge crowd had come to accompany me. We should take a photo, I thought, to commemorate the event, as I'll never get this much attention again! But my teeth chattered when I realised that the situation was way too serious for any humour; I shut my mouth and kept my white teeth inside. After all, my teeth had cost me a fortune to fix. I wasn't about to lose them over a joke.

The officer, in a warm and confident roar, assured me that everything would be OK, and I believed him. I never saw him again. As soon as we arrived, his colleagues took over and his mission was accomplished. Argos: it came to me. The one with a hundred eyes. Only a few ever look away; while they rest, other eyes take over.

I couldn't understand how they found out about the cell I'd belonged to in my early teens. Nor did I comprehend why I had become a threat to state security when all I had done was throw some rocks and Molotov cocktails at a police station. Burning bottles. Their noise more potent than any damage they might cause.

I denied absolutely any relation to Husam and the others. But they showed me his written confession on a paper they placed before my eyes. It had all our conversations, the places we frequented, everything. I realised I had to bet on time. I knew they wouldn't detain me forever, but betting on time was still risky, because my body was giving out.

They deprived me of sleep for two days. It felt like a lifetime. I had never felt the importance of sleep before. 'The Sleep Thief' is what one of the interrogators called me. I used to catch them unawares and sleep for a few seconds. Just a few seconds that sufficed to regain my energy for minutes, or sometimes an hour.

I'd never liked black, but when they placed that fetid hood over my head, I knew I would hate the colour forever. They used to swarm and encircle me. Their shoes made loud noises, loud as hammers, one after the other, hammering nails into my head. When the clangour of one nail was over, another began, and when that came to rest inside my head they would pull it out and put it back and hammer again.

Why don't they kill me? Why don't they kill this body? I have to persevere. Persevere against them. But my body kept shaking. I sat naked with the black hood covering my head like an idiot. How did my naked body look as I sat on the cold chair? Such absurd thoughts weighed my head down. It felt so heavy that it seemed as though it was about to fall off my neck.

'We will you put you under the table so you can listen to Husam's confession and the evidence he'll provide against you and the others. You'll sit under the table, spread your legs, and I'll put my foot on your testicles. If you utter one word, if Husam realises you are there, I'll castrate you. No one will save you from me.'

The interrogator said that. His bulging blue eyes were jumping their sockets to swallow me. Why did I comply? I should have refused.

Husam confessed. Is that important? I muttered silently. Why was I listening to his confession? Surely they have more advanced methods, ones that don't involve hiding me under a table. It seems that while he was studying in Poland, Husam blabbered to a young man from Ramallah. He bragged about his heroics. Was I pissed off with him? No. I couldn't be. Even though he was the reason we all went to prison.

Another morning came. One in which I could wash so as not to offend the guards' feelings, eyes and noses. They were going to take me to stand before the just judge and to sit next to the seasoned attorney, who was going to prove beyond a shadow of a doubt that these were just juvenile acts. All I had to do was apologise and show contrition for what I had done.

I felt warmth seeping into my lips when I saw the edges of Haifa's sea through the smudged windows of the car taking me to court. We entered the courtroom. Stacked eyes followed every motion of mine. Lips moved at a strange speed, emitting unintelligible sounds. My father had hired one of Tel Aviv's best attorneys to defend me. But I grew tired of his insistence that, for the sake of a reduced sentence, I apologise and show contrition. Looking at his mouth I could only see teeth and tongue. They moved like a saw, up and down, emitting an exhausting snore of useless sounds.

The prosecutor spoke a lot, and, like a choppy cassette tape, words slipped from his mouth and were scattered. Letters reverted to their origins and fell to the ground, rolling and bumping one another, their noise piercing my eardrum.

Till suddenly they stopped falling. I saw the judge's mouth speaking to me and there was quiet. I realised that it was my turn to speak. I must make my case. All eyes were on me, and fingers too, as without exception they pointed at me with the forefingers of their right hands, while their left hands rubbed circles on their bellies. They were laughing.

I felt a chill that July morning, as I grasped the gravity of that moment, as I wished I could grasp it forever. I wanted to say something grand. Something of such consequence that everyone would leave the courtroom to ponder it; they would form circles outside to discuss the human rights of people who look like us. I expected that one group would agree with what I said, while another would strongly disagree. But they would all appreciate the brilliance of my statements and the person who uttered them.

None of this happened. I was so tired. I still had to pick up the shards of my soul, which they had crunched underfoot. Plus, the judge was in a hurry. Perhaps he was thinking of packing his bags to go to Paris for a vacation, or of visiting an art exhibition?

All I had to do was apologise. That's what the attorney repeated a thousand and one times. That's what my mother said as well, when my father asked her to. 'No matter where we go and what we become, we'll still be Arabs. You must understand this. Even if you become a lawyer, a doctor or whatever. Even if you became God, you'd still be an Arab God, and of lesser value to them. A mere Arab!'

The judge repeated the question. 'Do you have anything to add to your attorney's statement?'

I shook my head and looked for my father's eyes in the courtroom. I looked long into his honey eyes, which verged on green. They were so gorgeous. But, God, why were they clouded in red? As if he hadn't slept for forty days. He'd aged so much. Or had he always looked like that? I wanted to say a lot to him, but he looked stunned by my behaviour. I felt both anger and pity for that generation, for those born around 1948, in Haifa or in any place related to it.

The judge's gavel resounded, declaring a year and a half of prison time. I heard drums in my ears, and suffocated ululations came out of hoarse throats.

My heart laughed and I did too. I laughed so hard my shoulders were shaking, and my lungs could breathe. Did I care why my body was full of noise, why drums were still beating in my ears? I was going to glimpse the sea on my way to prison. Through the car's smudged window? But I would see it still.

I was so free. I was so free when they put me behind bars.

SHAHIN

'Four kilos of berries for ten! Don't miss out. Ma'am! Sir! Come buy! I wanna go home.'

The vendors' screams in Hebrew were fighting fiercely to occupy the ears and minds of those walking through Ben Yehuda Market in West Jerusalem. Hoping they would drag their feet to this or that stall. Their husky voices were more potent than normal ones, like they'd been born with extra cords in their throats. I frequented that market every Friday. Swaggering as I carried my legs, even though they could barely carry me. I was a night owl, after all, and was only out in the daytime when necessary.

The screams curled round my head like a spray of bullets, their echoes overlapping in my ears. On Fridays, people stocked up on the vegetables they needed for the weekend, but they often bought more than enough for a whole week, as if war was imminent and provisions soon to be scarce. When stench sneaks into the nose the day becomes more treacherous. Sweat; a new style of cologne. Do they smell their own bodies, I wonder. Or do they prefer to bathe in cheap cologne instead of water? Their heavy scent walking before them.

Just thinking about the market gives me a headache.

'Ahmad dear! Please pay attention to the fruit you're picking for me.'

I said it hastily, as if speaking a language unrelated to Arabic. He was in the habit of looking at me in brief glances only, so others would not suspect preferential treatment. Always trying to hide behind his smile so that his Arabness was unexposed. I took the bag of berries. I worried that Mosheh, the owner, would hear me speaking Arabic at length. That would annoy him and arouse some fear among his customers. So our whisperglances imparted what Ahmad and I wanted to say. Today in particular, I wanted the berries to be the best of the best, because I was going to see Shahin.

He used to sell pencils on Ben Yehuda Street, near the market. There were many vendors, but something about him in particular stayed with me, and he was often present in my thoughts. Maybe his calmness reminded me of myself, when I used to go around Haifa's houses selling avocados. I was Shahin's age then, between thirteen and fourteen, dragging my shadow along for company through the neighbourhoods of Haifa. I hated knocking on doors asking if people wanted to buy what I was selling.

Shahin and other vendors like him went around the café tables. Each sold merchandise out of crammed plastic bags that swayed behind their backs, bumping them fondly from time to time, small bumps to pat and console. They chose merchandise that wasn't too heavy for backs that had outpaced age. Napkins, dishcloths, gum. Shahin was the only one who sold pencils.

When they were outside, between cafés, they went back to just being kids, playing and horsing around. Inside, they put on the mask of their trade. Even when the café owners kicked them out or the customers refrained from buying, the young vendors stuck close to their laughs, laughs that waited for them or roamed outside. Only laughs took them back to their real age, if just for a few seconds.

The vendors were all quite persistent, except for Shahin. But café customers couldn't tell him from others. They would look at him from a distance as his hand, tired from carrying pencils, extended across someone else's table. Some would try and get rid of him by flagging down a waiter, as if a waiter could save them from Shahin's extended hand. But the waiters were consumed by ongoing struggles on multiple fronts, one with empty plates waiting to be picked up from tables, another with those that were full and didn't like waiting in the kitchen; a third was with customers and their steady stream of special requests. All this left little time for waiters to kick the Arab kids out.

His Hebron accent gave him away. He was young and Hebrew stammered between his teeth. His mouth lost the few phrases his fellow sellers or his handler had taught him; he could not find the places between mouth and tongue in which confident Hebrew was formed. Even though his skin was fair and his eyes were green, customers only saw the dark features of his face.

He once said to me: 'Had I been the shade of a cloud they would've looked up and into my face deeply. I wish I were a cloud's shadow.'

For Shahin, cafés did not consist of tables, but rather eyebrows. Arched, joined-up and heavy eyebrows. Arched on purpose with displeasure at his approach; arched to express disinterest in his bundles of pencils.

When he went to bed, Shahin didn't have to count to one hundred to fall asleep. He drowned in a sea of joined eyebrows crashing against his face. Fatigue struck every part of his body.

Unlike other sellers in West Jerusalem, his persistence was short-lived. Shahin's clothes were wrinkled but always clean; his dignity bestowed some elegance on them. He buttoned his shirt all the way to the collar. Baggy trousers hid behind a belt whose last hole was made by a screwdriver or something like that, something sharp, anything to close that belt around his skinny waist and protect his trousers from dropping. His sneakers looked tired from long distances. Despite Shahin's attempts to wipe them with wet paper towels, their greyness paled with mud, and too with debris from those saliva-wet towels, which always stuck.

I used to love avocados. The day I started selling them I couldn't stand their taste any more. I hated them. Going around selling gave me nightmares.

'Gharib, darling, you have to go and sell avocados. The money your father makes doesn't cover our expenses.'

'I don't wanna sell anything. It's embarrassing to go around houses. Plus, if my schoolmates see me, they'll make fun of me. I don't wanna be like the kids from refugee camps.'

'You're not so special. You think you are better than those refugee kids? What we sell to the state doesn't cover the pickers' wages and your father can't work more than he already does. Can't you see that his back is crooked because he worked in construction for so long? What do you want? You want me to go around houses to sell?'

My mother guilt-tripped me and knew I wouldn't be able to keep resisting. What were we supposed to do, when my father was working day and night to make sure my older siblings could go to college? There were hardly any scholarships for Arabs. We owned ten donums of land planted with avocado trees, but were forced to sell them wholesale to the state at the low price it imposed. So to make money we used to steal our produce and sell it directly.

I hated avocados and squandered the little my mother gave me to spend in exchange for my work. At doors I was overtaken by shyness and my heart would race whenever I knocked and heard the approach of footsteps. I was afraid that I'd see one of my classmates or teachers.

I extended my hand to shake his and asked him his name.

'Shahin. My name is Shahin.'

There was a glitter in his eyes, wondering what brought me to this side of Jerusalem. Shahin! I thought, though I kept my thoughts to myself, why don't you take off this heavy jacket of a name, and come back in five years when you are big enough to carry it again? Your name is heavier than your age.

Shahin was staring at me and asked me in his hesitant Hebrew if I wanted to buy a bundle of pencils.

'Why are you speaking Hebrew to me, Shahin? I am a Palestinian like you from the north. My name is Gharib. I live and study here in West Jerusalem. Where are you from?'

'Hebron.'

'You come here every day to sell pencils?'

'Not every day. Twice a week. My father is in prison and I have to help my mother.'

Shahin's neutral face made me doubt the veracity of his words. But I reproached myself for my doubt, and in fact didn't care whether his words were true or not. I decided to believe what Shahin would tell me because I wanted to. I don't know how many thorns were stuck to his clothes. I didn't want to know if he avoided stepping on flowers when he crossed the border to Jerusalem. Did soldiers look at him through the barrels of their machine guns? Ready to blow away his little head at any moment? What did he think then?

My mother used to say that my big brown eyes and long eyelashes appealed to women despite my young age. They would buy what I had to sell. I also had a way with words and gave the impression that I was very knowledgeable. I had made sure I knew the difference between the three types of avocados I was selling and would explain them, adding enough advice to reassure my customers about buying fruit that was still unripe. If you wrap them in newspaper and put a banana peel between them, they'll ripen quickly!

I don't know if my advice was useful, but the women were convinced. What advice could Shahin give to his customers when he could barely speak their language? What would he say? Write history with my pencils? Write letters to your loved ones with these pencils?

Shahin was selling pencils to Israelis, but I had sold avocados from my father's land to Palestinians. Was that the difference weighing on my mind? When I saw Shahin being kicked out of the café I frequented, it felt like knives cutting.

Did they detest Shahin because he was an Arab, or because he was poor, or both? Did they simply want to drink their coffee in peace and that's all there was to it? Nothing to do with skin colour or creed, perhaps. I got mixed up back then. I couldn't always distinguish what I saw from my interpretation of it.

I remember that hot summer noon very well. Heat had stabbed its fangs into midday and I, a child back then, was walking next to my father, measuring and comparing my tiny shadow to his and wondering when mine would be the taller. We were crossing the corner by our house when a Russian kid yelled at us in Hebrew: 'Here come the dirty Arabs!' I picked up my pace and hurried towards home. My father's shouting froze me. Yanking me back by my shirt, he stuck his face against mine. I couldn't breathe. I used to have shortness of breath and suffocated easily. 'This is the last time you let anyone call you a dirty Arab. Go back! Answer him! Get your revenge!' The saliva flying out of my father's mouth at that moment bothered me more than the Russian calling me dirty. I thought how, despite having lived here for years, this so-called newcomer still couldn't speak Hebrew well and it was obvious. I told myself that maybe he didn't know that 'Arab' is not necessarily related to 'dirty'. Maybe he thought it was all just one word? I couldn't share this thought with my father. I breathed a sigh of relief when the Russian disappeared. As a child I couldn't stop rubbing my skin and it became reddish. Perhaps I was removing some dirt I didn't know existed. I used to stand in front of the mirror to compare my skin before and after bathing to see if it had lightened. A few years later, I started to go to the sea so that my skin would be more tan.

'Do you want to buy pencils?' Shahin asked hurriedly, as if frustrated by how scattered I seemed.

'Yes, give me a bundle. You come here every day?'

'No. Thursdays and Fridays. I already told you.'

Shahin's friends stood a stare's length away, their eyes fixed on us. When we took too long they leant on one another's bodies, on their toes to follow our conversation, their heads bobbing like wooden marionettes, their strings moving them with ease.

Shahin and I met every week by unspoken agreement. I would worry if he didn't show up. I became a permanent customer. His pencils were stacking up on the desk in my room. I moved them to an empty shelf, which quickly filled up too. The rubber bands wrapped the bundles and kept them fixed and stacked. They couldn't be easily moved. The questions I had about Shahin and his life piled up too, week on week; but he didn't like to answer. I only heard him say my name once, when he first asked me about it.

'Gharib. *Gharib*!'

Did he think it strange that I had such a name, or was he just repeating it to help himself remember? The first seemed normal enough; it was the second that expressed surprise. But I didn't ask about it. Why would I?

It seemed that I was going to just keep buying pencils, though if I did carry on, there would be no space left in my room for my own feet.

I even thought of making beds and chairs out of pencils,

but had yet to devise a method to make them sturdy and strong. If the furniture appealed to my friends maybe it could become trendy. I would find a talented carpenter in Hebron to help me devise my method, and it would be a great opportunity to visit Shahin's home and see where and how he lived . . .

I was deep in thought, staring at nothing, when a small hand touched my shoulder, accompanied by a shy but blooming smile. Shahin! Who else? I decided not to buy pencils any more. I decided, without knowing that I had, just to give Shahin the cost of the pencils and help him and myself.

When I gave him the money and the pencils back, and told him I wouldn't be buying anything, his fingers stammered as he put the money in his pocket. He took his hand out of his pocket but the note was still in his soft fingers. The smile fled from his face. I was the reason.

'I'm not a beggar.'

He said it. Each word had to drag the next out of his mouth, but he said it eventually. His eyes hid behind a sea of tears that never fell. What had I done, and what could I do now? I'd said what I'd said, and my words had wounded your smile. I didn't know – I, who used to sell avocados – how my sentence would wound you. I should have been the first to know. But I wasn't thinking of you. I was thinking of your pencils, stacking up in my tiny room. I want to rest, Shahin! Because I'm tired. I'm tired too!

'I'm sorry, Shahin!' I said. 'I didn't mean it. I respect your work and know you are not a beggar. I used to go around selling stuff just like you. I want to buy your pencils and support you. And I want you to know that I don't give money to beggars, and you aren't one. Please forgive me and give me a bundle.'

The ten-shekel note was wet in Shahin's fingers. He didn't say a word. He placed the bundle on the table and left. When he left the café, his laughs, which usually waited for him outside, had gone too. I can't remember his laugh, but stuck in my memory like colocynth are the tears he never let fall.

What I had feared came to pass. I knocked at the door of my geography teacher. His daughter's head appeared with two looped braids on each side, as if she were carrying bells with her head, waving them whenever she spoke. She looked like an idiot. I knew her very well, because she went to my school. Her father used to take her there hand-in-hand and would stand by her classroom, waving, until he was sure she'd gone in. Then he went to teach his own classes. I hated him. So when I saw him, way behind his daughter's braids, stretched out on a wooden bed, I felt like I'd been electrocuted.

I snatched my shadow and ran the half-hour back home. When I'd made it back with my basket half-empty, I threw it on the floor. The avocados danced as if they were trying to escape their black plastic bags. I rolled over on my bed and didn't talk to anyone.

The next day the teacher talked about avocados. But only my body was there. I was deaf, and imagined myself an avocado stone placed in water. We used to do this with avocado stones and watch the yellowish white roots sprout and later green shoots climb everywhere on the walls. He was talking about avocados and maybe ridiculing me, but I was a silent plant surrounding his neck.

Friday dragged its feet, but it arrived eventually.

I bought lots of berries. The silent looks I exchanged with Ahmad were whispers to make sure he picked me the best. They yell so much at Ben Yehuda Market, and, for that matter, in all of Jerusalem's markets, it almost bursts my eardrums. I only get up early in the morning when it is necessary, and even when I do, sleepiness still colours my lids.

Everything is a fight! Why does it seem to me that this country is in a constant fight? Everything around me is warring. Even calmness itself seems to be fighting, looking for a place of its own, and words are like shots fired from the barrels of human mouths in battle.

I decided to buy all of Shahin's pencils. In return, he could come to visit me for an hour or two. Maybe I could help him with his studies, play football, anything. I hoped he would agree. Carrying the bags full of berries and other vegetables, I went straight to the café so as not to catch only his shadow.

My footsteps were outpacing my heartsteps, which were racing to catch up. The further I was from Mosheh's stand, the louder his voice was in my ears, as if I were coming nearer instead of leaving the stand behind.

I was eager to see Shahin and his rare smile once I gave him the good tidings. I didn't have a clear plan: how long would I go on buying pencils? For the moment, I thought, everything could go on like this forever, and the word forever would comfort me. Yet I couldn't breathe at the thought of our situation going on forever. What if the gods did pinch one moment and repeat it eternally? Which moment would they choose?

I tripped and fell. I didn't know how.

People were running around haphazardly, not knowing where they were headed. Any ill-fated step might take one towards the silence of a waiting bomb, or a suicide bomber about to detonate. No one asked how people got to the point of silently blowing themselves up. No one will ask. There were many explosions in Jerusalem in those days. I came quite close to several. Once I overslept and didn't take the early-morning bus to college, and a Palestinian blew himself up on it. I should have been on that bus. Would I have recognised him? Felt his presence? Would he have known that I was a Palestinian like him? Would he have told me to get off? Would he not care? I was close to bombings many times, saved only because laziness and sleep had overstayed their visits. I was late to classes and survived. Had I been killed, I would have been counted by the Israelis as one of their dead. I didn't like that thought.

When the sound of an explosion reaches your ears, but you are still alive, it means you're not hurt, or that your injury hasn't killed you yet.

'A terrorist blew himself up! A terrorist blew himself up!' yelled someone with horror all over his face. I thought of Ahmed, the worker at Mosheh's stand, hoping he would hide to avoid being attacked and beaten by an angry mob who blamed him for the explosion. Even though he himself could have been one of the injured.

I rushed to the café where Shahin would be. My legs barely able to carry me. I don't know how I made it. I ran. Others were running too, but I was afraid that they would catch Shahin and beat him up. Or maybe he was among the dead?

When I reached the café there was screaming, but it was the sound of the explosion still resonating in my ears. The place was full of people but devoid of everything. Everything was devoid of life. So much blood flowing so easily. Everywhere.

People were moving and yelling like puppets on a TV screen, yet I couldn't change the channel or turn the TV off. I couldn't find Shahin among them, or among the corpses. I breathed a sigh of relief and sat on the pavement, waiting.

Shahin's heavy name was not among the names on the news, any news.

Nor was Shahin's house demolished as part of the collective punishment, but he never came to Jerusalem again. I wonder if he got lost travelling those distances. I wish he had given me his address.

I waited for him Friday after Friday, but the days were hollow except for his memory. As if I had never met him or had dreamt it all.

AIRPORT

I decided to take advantage of the freedom given to me by a passport premised on my own remains. I was to travel to Cyprus for a weekend. My Israeli passport allowed me to go there, and to Europe, without a tourist visa. I would have preferred to go to Beirut, because it is Beirut. Or to Ramallah, but Ramallah was closed off by military order, and for Israeli passports Beirut makes no exceptions, my Palestinianness notwithstanding.

I opened the door of the travel agency in French Hill right next to campus. It was full of Israeli students and I was amazed. Where did they get the money to travel? I often heard them whining about their budgets, whether or not they came from rich families or were on army scholarships.

Before I went to university, our financial situation was tough. My father had been working so hard for so long that he was drained. My brothers, Na'im and Hasan, had finished their studies and got married soon thereafter. Their family lives were saddled with expenses and I didn't want to add to their burdens. There were barely any scholarships for Arabs and a prerequisite for all of them was serving in the Israeli army. Very few Palestinians do. I had to work hard to pay for my tuition, so one year took two. I felt bitter whenever I returned home after a long day of work and study to hear speeches on the radio or TV that called on us to persevere, as if perseverance consisted of slogans alone. Could perseverance itself persevere? When I saw the halls at the Hebrew University named for the donors who paid for them, I felt jealous, like an orphan who knew his lineage but had no one to pat him on the shoulder at the end of the day, no one to ease his burden. Then again there is a sense of freedom in being orphaned. There are no guardians. Such was the case of Palestinians inside. Perhaps my parents named me Gharib to signify this estrangement I felt at home. The name describes me, but sometimes I forget that it is mine.

I waited forty minutes for my turn. The travel agent was of Moroccan descent, but the French accent in her Hebrew annoyed me. As if she was fiercely denying her Moroccanness. That's how I read her insistence on cramming a French word into every other sentence. I didn't ask her if she knew any Arabic; instead I extrapolated without enquiring. I didn't bother with her past. Those days her past had no place, either in the travel agency or in my concerns.

The travel agent didn't argue with me when I indicated that I would only travel on Cyprus Airways and not the Israeli El Al. She treated me normally and understood my name right away. Flying out of al-Lud Airport is exhausting and humiliating for Palestinians. They inspect every item in your suitcases, even a pin. I didn't like having my clothes and belongings brought out in front of employees and other travellers. I didn't like it done in a side room either. Nor did I like having an instrument comb my pants in front of everyone. Travelling on El Al increased the chances of having to go through all this. That was one of the reasons why I avoided them.

The dorms were ten minutes away. I walked back and started packing some clothes, sneakers, a toothbrush and toothpaste, soap, and Ted Hughes's *Crow*. I liked that book and had decided to write my paper on it. I felt his crow hovering over us and it didn't wish to leave. In vain I searched for a country where the crow was welcomed as a good omen, the way that Norway welcomes the owl. I wanted to find a myth that would debunk our crow-pessimism. I wanted to feel comforted as I looked at the crow in admiration. But I had to give up my admiration for the sake of myth: despite myself, I feared the crow as a herald of bad things to come, and would throw things at them to scare them off.

I packed my things in a small bag and closed the door, heading to the airport.

I would have three hours to kill at the airport, but I wasn't worried, since security was going to be so tedious and exhausting that the time would likely kill itself. I stood in line with everyone else. When it was my turn, a woman with serious, but neutral, features asked me about my bag and my reason for going to Cyprus. Another employee came and repeated the same questions but was nicer. And it was over!

I thought there must have been some mistake. I went up to the first woman and told her I was an Arab, perhaps she hadn't realised, so she was welcome to follow procedure and search my bag and every item in it, or take me to a side room so her colleague could search me after asking me to undress and using the wand all over my body. But she didn't get what I was trying to say. She told me the procedure was over and I could go and spend time shopping or do whatever I wanted.

It was like my identity was a coat they had stripped off on a cold day. Being searched, humiliated and deemed suspicious had become such fundamental parts of me that I couldn't live without them, though I'd always demanded they be stopped. Waiting for two hours, like any average citizen at their country's airport, was a strange and unfamiliar feeling. I was struck by how odd the phrase sounded to me: like any average citizen in their country. My country? Yes! My airport? Yes. But not my government, not my flag, not my symbols, not my passport. Not, not, not! Being an average citizen who causes no suspicion and is not guilty by association was something I had never experienced in public spaces. And definitely not at the airport.

The watch's arms were ticking monotonously, normally, and I was able to go from one place to the other without any problem.

There are two types of searches at airports. The usual one consists of questions about who packed your bags, whether you were given anything by anyone else, and your purpose of travel. The second type starts with: 'Take your bag and come with me, please.' At times the 'please' goes missing. That means they'll take you to the side room to search your clothes. They might also search you after asking you to undress. Upon finishing you cannot move around alone in the airport. There will be someone accompanying you. Saying goodbye to family can only take place hastily and from a distance. If you are stubborn and insist on saying goodbye up close, you're made to feel like you're stealing kisses, and you still do it in a hurry. You kiss your loved ones with the security person right next to you counting every brush of lips and repeating monotonously 'We have to go!' It will be odd to hear him use the word 'we', as if your fates were tied together. After you snatch that goodbye, snatch it as you do with all of life's lovely moments, he will continue to hover above you like the angel of death, reminding you that one day you must die. Not until you reach the booth to have your passport stamped do you leave and he leaves, returning to his work and his next prey.

This was the norm when I travelled, just as it is for many Palestinians when they travel, or even cross the border to Jordan or Egypt. That day I went to the airport alone. It was a normal weekend that didn't call for goodbyes and tears. I'd be back before I knew I'd left.

What to do? A woman was calling for passengers travelling to Cyprus to begin boarding. Everything was normal. There must have been a mistake. I couldn't stand normality or get used to it. Now fate had surprised me. I'd become a normal person who was neither interrogated nor looked at in disgust. Maybe it was just a coincidence. Nevertheless, I couldn't travel after all this normal treatment. I went to the ticket counter and asked to cancel my trip. The woman was surprised, but she apologised respectfully to say I would not get a refund. I was able to retrieve my bag at the last minute; I took it, growling.

I headed for the line of taxis, drivers waiting patiently at the rank, and threw my bag in the back seat of one and got in and slammed the door.

The driver was listening to Fairuz. He turned down the music as soon as I got in, but raised the volume again after I spoke to him in Arabic. The road to Jerusalem was empty except for a handful of cars. The closer we got the higher we went. 'It's beautiful, Jerusalem. Very beautiful!' he said and smiled. 'Yes, very beautiful. It suffocates us very much, but it is very beautiful.' We started a conversation about my trip. After I told him what had happened, he kept laughing, talking to himself and hitting his forehead with his palm. I fell asleep and woke up when we had reached the dorms. I heard him say:

'My dear Don Quixote, we're in Jerusalem. Here you go.'

HAMSA

I stretch out on my bed and shut my eyes. I hope to never open them again. Outside the window, birds are singing, as they have since time immemorial, paying no attention to those who hear them, to those who became refugees, or to those who stayed to become strangers in their own homes. Everything on this earth betrays.

This is our moment, but it will vanish in a moment too. Will the end of the day mark the last day in this house? Everything in nature but us is dancing its eternal dance. We dance fearing departure, separation and betrayal.

I open my eyes a second time, a third, so many times I lose track. When I am able to count, my eyes will have shut for good. Yet any such time would be a while from now, it seems. Whenever I open my eyes, my fingers are still holding Hamsa's wine-red scarf with interwoven silver threads.

Did she forget to take it, or had she left it on purpose? I don't know. She liked to adorn her body with it and would sleep on my bed like a carefree Canaanite goddess. Did I tie her wrists with it a night or two before she left? It doesn't matter. She won't return this time. She left no slip of paper with a line or two, as she used to. *Kisses. I miss you. See you this evening. Don't look at other women, the birdy will tell me. Love you love you love you.*

Hamsa is gone and the birds are still here, as are the white and coloured paper slips, the bills she used to find in the kitchen. She used to pen her words on their backs and stick them on the fridge door for me to see them when I woke up and went to the kitchen for coffee. Wait for me, I told her, but don't wait for me to promise you something. Yes, I do want to marry you, but not now. I can't now.

The last time we talked about the subject she drowned in silence, which was unlike her. Usually, she got very angry. A fire would break out in her body that could only be quelled by a waterfall of tears. This time was different. She asked me very calmly and reacted to my answer with even greater calm. When I asked her why she didn't want to say anything, she said all that could be said had been said already. And since my answer would not change, there was nothing for her to add. She fell silent, kissed me on my lips and slept.

I loved watching her while she was asleep. Her thin tan body naked. She often slept on her side with a hand under her head. Like an innocent child, or a philosopher who'd had a thought, just on the point of drifting off, and slept holding on to it. When she woke up in the morning and saw me looking at her, a smile would bloom on her lips and she would stretch in bed like a cat, trying to shake off sleep, but drowsiness would hold on to her until she showered.

I remember that morning in Jerusalem well. Rain was strumming the bedroom window. The first thing I saw were her dark-brown nipples upright. She was awake and looking at me and was toying with them, the wily smile on her lips that she had whenever she was aroused.

When I said good morning, she responded with a lustful smile. Blood rushed through my veins. I was late for my classes, but I couldn't resist. I never liked to let her down when she was brimming like a volcano.

I got out of bed and went to wash my face. When I came back, she was still toying with her nipples. I imagined milk bursting out at any minute and splashing my face. I kissed every opening pore the way one seeds a pomegranate – that was her phrase, how she described my kisses showering her warm body. I drowned in her, body and spirit. The smile of her soul stays with me even today.

She got up to open the window and came back to bed. She pulled up the covers and placed them between her thighs. In a voice that knew how much I loved her, she asked, 'Where is Fairuz and the coffee, habibi?' I never pampered anyone the way I did her, although I was and still am not a morning person. I was always in a bad mood and couldn't tolerate anyone, except her. She was coquettish and would do anything to see a smile sit on my lips. 'I love your smile. A lot. When I see it, I feel the whole world is mine,' she often said.

I challenged her once, when we were on our way back home from a coffee shop. I craved her and wanted to make love under the chestnut tree in 'Ayn Karim we always talked about. The night sky was silver. The moon lit our way like a genie, tracking us with her lamp. Every now and then a few flirtatious clouds blocked its light.

Hamsa hesitated a lot. I recognised the silence. Thoughts would wrestle in her head until either madness or stubbornness won. She only said one sentence – 'I'm all yours' – and then fell silent. I feared for her. That I would hurt her.

They chopped down that tree a week ago. I wasn't able to even bid it farewell. I was going back home and saw them putting its limbs into a machine that devoured it.

I lost the desire to stay in Jerusalem. I was suffocating, and decided to move to Tel Aviv. Jerusalem was so sacred to everyone that it had lost its sanctity as far as I was concerned. I couldn't walk down any of its streets without seeing or hearing a group trying to prove its existence. I was tired and didn't want to prove my existence: *I exist*.

I don't like Tel Aviv that much, though I also haven't really given it a chance. It feels fake and haughty, the way it lives on Jaffa's remains. It gobbled up Jaffa and left it to die. That is Tel Aviv: a city like all modern cities, lacking history, a city with no history beneath its ribs. I don't like cities like that. Tel Aviv is also a liar, because it had a history which it destroyed, claiming modernism and a zero-hour birth. There is no zero hour in this country. Every grain of sand has gallows.

I live on Ben Gurion Street, though I'd rather it was called al-Zahra or al-Rabi'. I don't know if I would have been more optimistic, but Ben Gurion does not appeal to me. Al-Zahra does.

You can only walk through the city's streets while holding hands with noise. Noise walks alongside you and never lets go. There is no respite. Car fumes and horns make the city look like an old hag, heavy make-up hiding the wrinkles on its face.

The fumes from buses and cars drain Tel Aviv's air. Its two blackened lungs have no hope of healing soon. I was waiting for the bus to take me to eat fish at one of al-Ajami's restaurants. My shadow disappeared under its front tyres; I hate it when someone, or something, steps over my shadow. As soon as I'd got on and paid, the driver soared, as usual, the bus nearly taking off in flight. I had to hold on so as not to fall over. I found an empty seat, sandwiched between three passengers. I didn't look at them until I sat down.

I hadn't seen her for more than five years. She was sitting across from me, eyes shut, her head leaning against the window. I couldn't believe my eyes. My heart raced so fast I thought it was about to pierce through my chest. She's right here! The last words I heard from her were 'Goodnight, habibi.' She never called after that. She changed all her numbers, left Jerusalem, and vanished. I looked but couldn't find her. I knew where her family lived. They were from Wadi al-Nisnas, in Haifa.

What did she want me to do once she had given up on me? To go to her family and ask for her hand? Would that have got us back together? I didn't. I was just out of prison. My family was drained and had suffered much. I didn't dare broach the subject with my father, because he was against the marriage. Hamsa had been in love with someone else before. It didn't matter to me, but it did to him. I couldn't confront him after getting out of prison. I asked her to be patient, but she stopped believing me. She was right. I don't know if I would have ever confronted my father. Maybe today I would. I don't know.

My father was stubborn and was disappointed in me when I went to prison. He didn't want us to dabble in politics and forbade us from going to protests. He believed that the only useful thing for us to do was to succeed individually and professionally. When I went to prison he cried and only visited me once. It was a sad visit. He didn't say much, but I saw, for the first time, the disappointment in his eyes to see me there. It didn't matter that it was for political reasons, or that some were calling me a hero. He didn't see this heroism of mine. The expense of hiring the best attorney had drained him even more.

I didn't like my father's logic and his way of seeing things. When I spoke to him about marrying Hamsa, his response was vulgar. I didn't say much back then. I was ashamed of his response and his stubbornness. I told myself that I would finish my studies in two years and that by then the past would be distant. He might change his mind. I cried that night when he said to me: 'You want to marry a used one?' As if Hamsa were a car or a gadget. I thought of my mother at that moment. I despised my father and his words, but didn't say anything. When Hamsa asked me if I had told my parents about us, I told her it wasn't yet time.

You are sitting before me now with your eyes shut. I look at your long fingers. My face still remembers your soft touch. God how I missed your fingers. I missed them when I was in prison. After I got out, I just wanted to be in your arms. The moment I saw those lips I was filled with joy and felt alive again.

I died when you were absent. I died. I only realised that I'd died when I saw you, because that's when I came to life again. I used to tell you this, but you didn't like to hear it. You no longer believed my words.

But my words were genuine. When you were absent my heart died. You said you wanted us to get married because that was the only bond that would let us live safely in this jungle of a world. I wasn't against that, but I couldn't stand up to my father. I was a coward. They broke my thorns!

You used to always tell me, 'It's OK, habibi. We have to tend to our thorns, just as we do our roses. Remember to tend to your thorns.' We could have gone on living like that, and I would have married you one day. Maybe not. Maybe you were right.

There was no ring on your hand. Does that mean you were not married? Even on the bus, you still slept like a smiling philosopher who has just figured out the universe's dilemma.

God, I love you so much. I didn't want to wake you up. I let you sleep. It was like you'd never left. The old man sitting next to you was tracking my looks, as they took in every part of your body.

Your skin was still soft and tan. When you open your eyes, I thought, I'm going to put my fingers on your lips and ask you not to say anything until I take you to the sea, hold you in my arms, and apologise. I'm going to tell you I miss holding you in my arms. That I'm alive again because I see so much of you, as I used to, when I look into your eyes.

I thought of reaching over and waking you up. Or leaning over and kissing you on your lips and forehead. But we were no longer together and I had no right to do so. Maybe you were in the middle of a lovely dream. I didn't want to interrupt it and upset you.

The bus reached Jaffa, right by al-Sa'a Square. Hamsa opened her eyes and saw her reflection in the window. Her eyes looked outside, searching for someone among the people at the bus stop. Perhaps someone she was going to meet? She turned to find her way out; she left touching her hair. I was frozen and didn't utter a word. As if my heart was bleeding. I kept looking at her, my tongue tied as I watched her standing at the bus stop. The bus moved. I thought she had glimpsed me and looked away. Pinning my face to the glass, I watched her disappear in the distance.

PARTY

I'd forgotten to inform my mother that I would be coming home over the weekend to visit. Usually there was no need to call since she was always there. Even when she went out, she would return before evening. She rarely slept elsewhere, except when visiting my sister Salma, in Ramallah, to stay with her if she's sick. When she went away for a long period, she would lock the door and leave the key in the mint pot next to it.

I was dying from the heat. The sun's rays had clawed their way under my skin. I felt like an idiot for travelling from Tel Aviv to Haifa in the middle of the day, when the heat showed no sign of retreat. Admitting that wasn't of any help as I went up the hill towards our house.

I opened the main gate with tired hands and closed it behind me. I saw the jasmine bush's branches were keeling over, declaring their need to rest. The key was in the mint; Mother was going to be gone all day at least. I called my grandmother, who told me that my parents had gone to visit Salma and were spending the night there.

I sat in the chair where I always felt protected. It was big and I could stretch my legs without taking anyone else's space.

My mother had the curtains closed all the way to make sure no dust entered the house. She was in an ongoing gruelling war with dust. It was an obsession. She and my father argued about that all the time. It seemed as if my father was jealous because the dust got more of her attention than he did.

I felt suffocated in the living room, so I went out to the balcony. Some of the neighbours' faces looked at me like mice sniffing around the area. I preferred the living room and its shut curtains to that, so I went back in, looking for any dust particles my mother had forgotten to remove.

The phone rang. I ignored it. It kept ringing. It must be important, I thought. Will I feel stressed if I miss it and keep wondering who it might have been? I guess I have to get it. What a drag, I thought. I got up to answer.

It was Dany, my old neighbour in 'Ayn Karim. I hadn't seen him since I left Jerusalem more than a year ago. I taught him how to smoke a water pipe and drink arak over long evenings that would end in arguments about politics. Or about the conservatives who had started to tighten the noose around him too. The first time I went to visit his family home in 'Ayn Karim I couldn't breathe. It was a quiet town. Its stone houses had two or three stories with vaulted windows. The buildings were all that had remained, along with one Palestinian family who had been displaced from Iqrit. I kept silent most of that evening. Ghosts were jumping around me. I cried after I left his house.

'Hello Gharib.'

'Hi Dany. How are you? It's been a while.'

'I tried calling you in Tel Aviv many times and then I thought I'd try you at your parents'. I'm leaving for England and want to invite you to a farewell party at my place. I'm living in a beautiful house in 'Ayn Karim, not far from where we used to live. But this house has a different history. I'll tell you all about it when I see you. Bring some Arab music! And are you ready to make some tabbouleh if I buy all the ingredients? I'll help! What do you say?'

'I don't know, but give me the address.'

I wrote down the address and felt my ribcage crush my breath. I went into my room. It had stayed the same since I left for college. Its walls still had photographs and posters from film and theatre festivals in Ramallah, Jerusalem or Tel Aviv. I used to go to them when I was at college, but there was no place for posters in my dorm room, so I brought them here. The paint on the wall was still off-white, as it had been since my childhood. An old man's face disappeared behind a poster's right corner. One of the four pins holding it had fallen. I didn't look for it or try to pin the edge back. Maybe I didn't want to see the old man's face. It was a popular poster that I had seen on many a wall. I'd bought it myself. But I grew tired of seeing that old man's face. It pained me to see him carrying Jerusalem like a rock on his shoulders. I lay down on my stomach and slept deeply.

When I woke up the sun had set. I got up, took a shower, and felt fresh. I shaved, put on some cologne, and wore jeans and a maroon shirt. I called my brother Na'im to borrow his car. I locked the door behind me and put the key in the mint pot and went to my brother's. I took the car keys and drove to Jerusalem.

Fairuz's voice filled the car. I looked for a neutral song. Fairuz doesn't have that many neutral songs. Each of her songs holds a memory and a reminder of how time passes. I found one: 'Kifak Inta' Not that it didn't hold a memory, but the memory it held I didn't recall. Sometimes I have such a surplus of memories. Maybe I should start a business and export them?

I drove along the seashore, sporting a smile, and felt ecstatic. I touched my lips. Why was I so aroused? Was it because I was on my way to a party? I'd gone to many parties without feeling this way. My smile on the glass of the windshield looked at me; I smiled back.

I looked at the sea and remembered Ghassan Kanafani's stories and the stories of those who boarded ships in horror. I kissed the sea goodbye and wondered if they had done so too, before remembering it was their cities they would have kissed. They were at sea.

Jerusalem's mountains were still far away when I left the sea behind in my rear-view mirror. The car reached Jerusalem's outskirts. I only needed fifteen minutes to get to 'Ayn Karim, which I knew well, because I had rented my first studio apartment there. All my memories with Hamsa were there. Hamsa, who kissed me on my lips, whom I'd never heard from since that day.

I don't like remembering street names, because each street has two: the one that is written, and the one warring with memory. Their names and ours. Even when one of ours and one of theirs are the same, the names still have a stolen taste. Names. I don't like that plural. When I utter it, I feel that I am without features. I thought a lot about going to some Greek island and claiming amnesia. No one would know anything about me. I could forget who I was. But this thought brought me no comfort.

I reached Dany's house minutes later. I climbed the three or four front steps. I used to feel awe when I visited an old house. Memories of what I had read and heard would swarm and take a hold of me. Sometimes this whole country seems like a stubborn ghost. I touched the door like a lost blind man, or a lover who had sneaked into his beloved's room and wanted time to stop as he touched her. The door was made of old wood with carved geometric shapes surrounding what resembled a pomegranate. The main door with its two shutters stood tall. It was pale brown in the evening light. An iron lion's head sat in the middle, its mouth biting a knocker. I moved it and waited, but no one answered.

I took a few steps back to check the address, to make sure I wasn't lost right here in the street I knew. It doesn't hurt to check again. I looked for a bell and found one to the right of the door. When I pressed it, it chirped like a flock of birds. It sounded artificial and jarring. Dany opened the door and welcomed me warmly.

He had beautiful eyes. Honey-coloured with some green, just like my father's. We went to the kitchen to make the tabbouleh, drink some wine and catch up. I didn't notice the other guests or bother to scrutinise the place.

The stereo was playing Um Kulthoum's 'Sirt il-Hubb'. Dany had memorised some of the lyrics when I translated them for him, one night after Hamsa's departure had scorched my heart. I'd carried a bottle of arak and some weed and we smoked until I felt my head exploding. I taught Dany the first two lines and he would remind me of them whenever we met and drank. We finished making the tabbouleh and left it in the kitchen to soak up the olive oil and lemon juice.

Dany was going around like a bee, talking and socialising with his guests. But alcohol had got the better of his concentration and he didn't seem to be following what they were saying. I, on the other hand, was a lost wasp, looking around the house. The house had a huge room in the middle whose doors led in all directions. There was only one high window, above an open door leading to a tiny garden, which I never would have noticed otherwise. I went out long enough to see an almond tree, a lemon tree, and mint and roses. Back in the main room, Édith Piaf was playing and those listening were swaying along. I stood in the middle, watching and sipping my glass of wine, now almost empty. I went to get more. It was a big house, one room inside another, like a magic box. Cigarette and water-pipe smoke saturated the air like cancer. Each room had a different type of music and lighting. I went into an eighties room and didn't like it; after having filled my glass (and taking the bottle along, so as to not have to go back), I went into yet another room, looking for a spot to sit.

This room only had the echo of the music next door. Guests who preferred chatting to dancing congregated in the centre. They were speaking various languages: English, German, French, and one group tried out its Hebrew. Most of them were foreigners who were working or studying in Jerusalem. I needed to sit down. I hadn't eaten anything since that morning. I looked with eagle eyes and found a spot next to a woman I could bet was French from the way she dressed. I was spot on. I apologised and asked if the spot next to her was vacant. She motioned for me to sit down with a seductive smile. Why had I apologised? I feel like I need to, always, and I do it for no reason. What were my most important apologies? What if I recorded them? Forget it, Gharib. Just start a conversation with her.

It was a relief to sit down. My head stopped spinning. Now the place itself was just spinning around me. A smile slipped through despite myself and I realised that I was getting tipsy even though I hadn't had that much to drink. My stomach yelled at me to feed it, but I didn't want to leave my spot right away, as the woman might misinterpret it. I looked into her eyes. They reminded me of Hamsa's and my heart started to race. I was sweating and felt a shiver. Though it was foolish and I knew it, I gulped the wine in my glass. The French woman raised her eyebrows. I moved closer and asked her what had brought her to this place. She said she was an exchange student for the year. I used the loud music as an excuse to inch closer and we started speaking into each other's ears. She talked about her reasons for choosing Jerusalem. She had a light perfume that I could only smell up close. It mixed with her body odour, and she smelt like vanilla.

My lips were close to her ears, but I didn't touch her. This aroused me and I realised that she knew how to play this game too. While her rose-coloured lips avoided brushing my cheek, she looked deep into my eyes as she finished her sentences. The glow in them overwhelmed me and an electric current radiated through my body. I remembered how Hamsa's eyes glowed when we made love and our bodies were locked together. This memory snuffed the lust out of my eyes. I excused myself and went to the kitchen, where I scooped a bare five spoons of tabbouleh. I took a bottle of mineral water and some bread and went out to the garden to eat in peace. The sour aftertaste in my mouth was slowly finding its way to my liver and melting it. Whenever I looked at the house, I felt my breath shorten. The question of its original inhabitants was hunkering in my mind.

The tabbouleh reminded me of the homeland. The olive oil had the scent of the Galilee. I wouldn't like to live there, but loved to visit. I am a son of the sea and we sea-children suffocate in the mountains. I felt a twang in my side again, as if my liver was hanging by a rope inside my body and threatening to fall.

I looked around me. The moon sat in Jerusalem's sky the way it always does. It might appear bigger or smaller, but it comes and goes on time, not giving a damn about whether we exist or not. A spectre squatted under the lemon tree. I walked towards it, using my imagination as a cane. It was surrounded by a bed of mint, like a dark-green carpet, not its usual colour. It was a woman who squatted; she was weeding the mint. I called to her. She didn't turn round and I didn't know if she heard me. She was weeding hurriedly. I reached down to tap her shoulder but couldn't touch anything. I tried again, like I wanted to grab her body, but my nails scratched the palm of my own hand instead. I couldn't believe what was happening. I grabbed her shoulder more forcefully, but my fingers slipped through her and again scored my palm. Yet I could still see her there, weeding. I kept trying. I thought I heard a voice singing, but it vanished.

Every grain of bulgur felt like a shard of glass in my stomach. I rushed to the bathroom and washed my face with cold water. I was afraid if I opened my mouth I would spit out my own blood. I closed my eyes and drank some water, then left. Everyone was jovial.

The place itself was the angel of death clutching my neck, but he would neither take me with him nor let me go. I headed to the door to leave. Dany saw and stopped me, as if sensing what was going through my mind. Consolingly he said, 'Look, this house was built in the Arab style, like the other houses in the area, because the owner wanted it to be aesthetically consistent. He truly admires and appreciates Arab culture, but he couldn't live here, so he left and sold it to the current owner, who kept it as is. So it's not like the other houses around here. Its owners were not displaced. Do you understand that, Gharib?'

Gharib left in a hurry without saying a word. He still felt like he was bleeding internally. He was afraid to open his mouth and spit blood. He opened the door and, as he was going down the steps, he tripped and fell. The ground, why couldn't it carry him? He was fidgeting. He rose up and tried to keep his head proud.

July had made it halfway. It was warm, but 'Ayn Karim's mountain weather sent a breeze through the open door. The guests saw Gharib fall. Some of them felt pity. Others found his behaviour odd. He looked around and saw people he recognised, all leaving hurriedly, looking scared. He stood up. He called out and he begged. He held on to them. But they didn't notice; they didn't hear. Their shadows were everywhere around him. He fell back on the ground and almost broke bones. A few guests craned their heads from the door and windows, looking.

Someone enquired: 'Who is that? What's wrong with him?'

One of the guests volunteered a response right away:

'No one. Just a Palestinian who had too much to drink. They don't know when to stop. He's had too much to drink. That's all there is to it.'

BREAKING THE FAST

The crackle from the loudspeaker of the mosque near our house usually drew more attention than the call to prayer itself. The imam used to fidget and move the microphone, and the scratch alarmed all ears.

The streets were empty at that hour. Ramadan was on its way out. The family sat around the table in the garden right under the grapevine. The vine covered the entrance and its bunches dangled like beautiful breasts I could toy with and reach up to pluck.

We were used to the crackle but we still all laughed loudly, except for Salma. Her laugh was usually the loudest; today it sounded crestfallen.

'What's wrong with you?' I asked her.

'Nothing. It's just what we talked about today.'

I didn't say anything. Any comment on my part would have started a conversation with others and I didn't want to ruin the moment.

My father sat in the middle. My mother, next to him, appeared to be worried when she heard me and Salma talking. Her body language resembled a question mark as she stared at Salma, as if to shush her. I laughed deep inside. My mother still thinks we're children who will be afraid and hide if she stares at us enough. Salma turned to contemplate the jasmine she had planted many years ago. Hasan and Na'im sat with their wives and children, crowding the rectangular table. Salma and I were each at a corner.

The loudspeakers stopped crackling and the imam declared that God was great. Bismillahs were heard around the table and the hands followed to fill plates. I imagined the bismillahs of the entire city rising at that moment to a crowded sky, where they would tussle to be the first in Heaven's ear. Does Heaven have just one ear, or many? One for each human?

The clinking of forks and knives predominated. Salma chewed on her silence, spat it out. Her tears rained on her food. She looked at my father who was eating too.

'I don't want to sign the papers.'

'Why?'

'I don't like the way you divided the inheritance.'

'I did give you half of what your brother gets. I also paid for your college tuition. I never deprived you of anything. What more do you want?'

'I don't want anything. But if you're going to give me something, I don't want half a share.'

'It's your share according to tradition. You'll get more than most girls here. Plus, it's my money and I do what I want with it.'

'You are free to do whatever you want, just as I am free to refuse to sign the paper, because I'm against it.'

'I always treated you right. This is pointless stubbornness.'

'OK, fine. From now on I'll love you half, and feel half the sadness, and only one eye will cry, and I'll recite half of the Fatiha over your grave.'

The silence swallowed me and everyone else. I got up and stood next to the jasmine bush. As I lit my cigarette and inhaled, I felt I had betrayed Salma. I hadn't said a word to back her. She was still sitting at the table, though she had stopped crying and was starting to eat.

LIKE THE FEAR OF THE DOT ON THE LETTER خ

In Arabic, fear is a three-letter word. But they are big and rough letters. The first of them, خ, or Khā', always looks like an alligator whose mouth is wide. I am the dot on top. The alligator sits lazily, doing nothing except waiting to devour me as soon as I fall.

Fear lurks and eats me from within. It spreads everywhere inside me. It turns ordinary objects into burdens that carry meanings greater than they can hold. There is no reason for my fear, nothing rational; I haven't done anything illegal since my imprisonment. So why do I feel that a catastrophe awaits whenever the phone rings? Or when I find an official letter in the mailbox?

Fear preys on me. It pierces my dreams and body and eats my bones just as rust does iron. I didn't expect it to sneak into my dreams nightly, turning everything I like into a nightmare.

I used to enjoy going to museums, and would be moved by anything I saw, really, any old object, a jar of clay. The thought that it had been touched by someone hundreds or thousands of years ago stirred my imagination and nostalgia without knowing why. What were they thinking when they made it? Doubtless, they were not thinking about how this water jar they drank from daily would eventually become a relic, or that visitors would stand before it in admiration and listen to the myths they call history.

I open the mailbox and find a letter whose paper is made from anemones. Anemones, together with death and the narcissus, were the first signifiers of my memory. The letter's lines look like petals, not like lines penned by a human. A month later these lines still surround me every night in my dreams.

Dear Mr Gharib Haifawi,

Greetings.

We hereby invite you to attend the opening of the new National Museum, tomorrow at 4 p.m. We will send a driver to pick you up at half past three. Please be on time.

Respectfully,

The Museum Administration

I throw the letter on the floor and avoid looking at it. Anemone leaves fall everywhere. They follow me and cover my face. I can't breathe. I suffocate but don't die. That's how the dream ends. In the rest of the dream I don't sleep. It is tomorrow. I find myself showering, combing my hair and waiting for the taxi.

I stand by the window. My cologne is too strong. Why did I even put it on? I don't want to go out. As soon as the driver arrives I'll go down and tell him to go away. That's what I say to myself in the dream. I won't go to any openings or museums I don't know about, or have never heard of. Who am I anyway to be invited to a museum opening?

The minute hand gnaws on the first half of the fourth hour of that May afternoon. In the dream it's always May. The days change but not the month. The taxi's tyres stop in front of the building just as the minute hand bites thirty. The driver gets out of the car and stands next to the rear door. He opens it and waits, his eyes fixed on the front of the building. He stands there. Hands clasped.

Two glassy eyes, a yellow smile and carefully combed, thin brown hair parted on the side. A frugal smile that leaves no wrinkles round the eyes. His manners and greetings are very proper, which makes me forsake my intention to ask him to leave. I sit in the back seat. He drives us without once looking in the rear-view mirror.

The man with the strange smile is silent. Every night I try to think of a topic of conversation to draw him out, but I'm tongue-tied and I don't utter a word. Nor does he. And the distance between us remains. Every dream is the same.

The travelling time is the same: exactly half an hour, during which I hear the arms of a clock knocking at my eardrums. I hear it even after I wake up. It strikes and strikes again and only stops when we reach the museum. The stranger drives the car silently until we reach a place along the sea. The car makes a turn. It parks in front of a building right on the shore. I don't remember ever seeing this building before, but it looks old, as if it has been standing there forever. He gets out of the car and says in a confident tone: 'Here you go. We have arrived.'

'Where?'

The stranger assures me that the museum opening is in that building on the shore. He tells me my family are there. I am surprised; I ask him what all this has to do with my family. He says little apart from assuring me that they live in this place. I get out of the car without paying him, and in fact I'm surprised that he asked me to pay, since the offer of the car service was theirs. I close the car door without looking at him. I climb the five wide steps and see a broad façade of coloured glass, with drawings of a historical nature. The glass door opens and two women welcome me. One is blonde, has green eyes, and her hair is tied back. She is wearing a black suit, the shirt underneath sky-blue, the hem of her skirt knee-length and embroidered in red the colour of blood and green the colour of cedar. The other one is dark-skinned with brown eyes and is wearing the same style of suit, albeit in white with slightly different embroidery.

Both sport wide smiles. Yellow smiles of the type I hate. These smiles never change in shape or duration. The blonde woman greets me with a voice feigning warmth.

'Welcome to our country's National Museum, the first of its kind in the world. We congratulate you on being a witness to this era. What you see here is that which remains of the old inhabitants of this land, going back thousands of years; they have preserved the traditions and customs of this country. This is something you will not find in any other place in the world. You will see that we are trying in every way possible to help improve their living conditions, so that as many of our visitors as possible may see this for themselves, before these people become extinct.'

I did not understand what the blonde woman was talking about. As she spoke, the brunette was nodding in stupid agreement with her colleague. I don't comment on these statements. I follow the blonde woman, who is walking confidently ahead of me. She opens doors, one after another, explaining the place's history and the museum's architectural features. We enter a vast hall, which could hold a thousand humans if they stood side by side like marks on a ruler. The floor is dark wood. In the middle stands a platform forty centimetres high. Each centimetre signifies one year of wandering.

On the platform there are automata of men and women busy doing artisanal work. In one corner there is a group of statues of women baking taboon bread. They light the fire under the stone and flip the dough back and forth in their hands, then place it on the saj as if they've been doing it forever. One loaf of bread after the other comes out and tourists stand in line to eat it.

The tourists fill the hall and contemplate these beings in awe. The taste of the bread impresses the first group; they applaud. Yet it is the computer engineer who designed and programmed the movements and memories of these bread-makers who receives the most applause and admiration.

The line to taste taboon bread gets longer. The scent of the bread seeps into my nose; I stand in line like other tourists to get a piece. When it is my turn the bread's scent is mixed with the scent of a body I recognise. I look at her eyes and vomit liquid, the aftertaste of coffee and cigarettes. Every night I feel this taste in my dream and every morning I find the aftertaste in my mouth when I wake. It's been a month. The tourists are disgusted and they turn round to stare, as do the statues. The female statue looks away. It's my mother, Alya. She looks in my direction, but not at me. She is baking taboon bread and I stand like a tourist to get it from her, but her eyes are lifeless and made of glass. She motions with her hand. Her hand tells me to leave.

I try to call to her, yelling from the core of my being, but I don't know how my voice will come out when my tongue is still tied. I try to untie it but I can't. I keep screaming and calling out wordlessly. The security guards grab me and drag me out and throw me in the garden.

There I find a walnut tree whose fruit is almost ripe, its green husks cracking and seeds falling. I take some of them and pick some of the mint planted around the tree. I bundle them together with fig and grape leaves, fifty-nine of them. I pick up a thick branch that has fallen on the ground and leave the garden. I walk until I get to a hill overlooking the sea.

I dig a hole in the dirt with my tired hands and see how they age as dirt hides under my fingernails. Just a few hours, and old age appears! I keep digging until I fall asleep, exhausted. By the time I wake the sky has put on its evening dress. I go back to the museum.

Alya is dead. Her eyes are lifeless. Alya is dead; life is snuffed out from her eyes. 'I'm afraid that when I die there'll be no grave for me in this country,' she used to say. Alya is dead and an object visited by tourists. She is dead, but the shell of her body is still there. They display her every day. They don't bury her. Is this the nightmare inside the nightmare? Her corpse rots on the inside, but they don't bury her. She stays there baking taboon bread. The bread she didn't even know how to make. She was from Haifa. City women don't make taboon. But she bakes it at the museum even while dead.

I feel weaker, but still walk to the museum and circle round. There are no guards or dogs. I go up the five steps and strike its door with the branch I carry as if it were one of my limbs. The glass door breaks; every evening, the shards scatter. Some of them hit my face and pierce my skin. I feel blood flowing, but when I touch my face there is none.

I approach the huge platform and find the statues sitting there. Only one of them has a shadow. I know it is my mother Alya, so I move closer. She is very thin. Her skin is ghostly white, and her body is cold. I carry her and she feels heavy even though she's actually light. I can see a smile on her lips. She died with a smile. Perhaps she knew I would come back to bury her.

I walk away with her every evening, every nightmare, and when I'm almost out of sight, I realise that their heads are looking at me, though I don't look back. I hear a voice calling: 'She waited long for you. When she saw you today, she regained her smile. Don't worry about where you will bury her, as long as she's facing the sea.'

I walk along the seashore until I am near the hill. I lay her down and undress her. I wash her head, hair and body with seawater. I kiss her forehead and pick her up. Water drips from her naked body and grains of sand fall. I reach the hill. I lay her down inside the hole and unfurl the bundle. I take the walnuts and their husks and rub her lips and eyes. I take the fifty-nine tree leaves and cover her body. I scatter the mint leaves in the air and say:

'I don't have perfume for your body, but the seawater and its sand will be your perfume. I rubbed you with the walnut you so loved and made it your kohl, the way we do to our dead. Mint will carry your soul wherever you desire. In lieu of a white shroud, these leaves will cover your body. I plucked fifty-nine leaves, for your years. The leaves that remained on the tree will keep your memory alive forever. You were an honourable mother in a land that did not honour you. We were made of dust and to the unknown you go. Only we will attend your funeral: I, the stars, sea waves and this moon.'

But I wake up every day before I can bury her. She remains a corpse next to her grave and I sweat. Every day I am visited by this nightmare, except yesterday. Opening the mailbox, I saw a letter just like the one I saw in the dream. After standing in shock, I took it and went up the stairs to my apartment. I left it on the desk, unopened.

ALYA CRIES

'Hello sweetie. What is your name? Is Baba or Mama at home? Tell them it's Auntie Alya from Palestine, from Haifa!'

The child on the other end disappeared. My mother had held it together. Soon thereafter, her cousin Hamdan, who sounded like he'd just woken up, got on the phone.

'Ahlayn, Alya. How are you, dear cousin, and how is my aunt?'

My mother broke down and cried as if just realising now that her mother had died. She'd been crying for three days, but in silence. It was the first time I saw my mother as a daughter. Not because she was crying, but because I could see, when her cousin asked about my grandmother, that she felt orphaned for the first time. Her mother. She cried and her body shook and she was about to suffocate so I took the phone. Hamdan was crying too, at the other side. He'd figured it out and was telling my mother: 'We are orphaned, now, Alya.' My grandmother was the last of her siblings; the others had all died in Jordan. She remained in Haifa after her family left in 1948. They fled to Jordan while bullets flew over their heads, as she used to tell us time and again. Her mother died on the way there. Ruben, her son, was carrying her on his back. He went on with his blind sister, Salma, and his brother Hasan. They disappeared with all those who disappeared. As the years passed, their shadows got bigger and bigger, like a giant's. They were far behind neighbouring borders, yet close like an illusion. As if about to return any minute and knock on the door. It is so difficult to relay news of a death over the phone. You embrace the sorrow, but nothing embraces you. Everyone realises what a tragedy it is to be in the diaspora. So cruel not to bid a loved one farewell. Both Hamdan and my mother were wailing. I was in the middle, between two people who had just been orphaned. I hadn't realised how tough it would be to be an orphan at sixty.

My mother's languid eyes wilted. She cried like never before. I'd seen her cry, of course. My father made her cry a lot. He had joie de vivre and wanted to live life to the fullest, but he didn't like how she complained about matters of no concern to her. She was tense and would get upset if one of us, her children, moved an object. Looking at her now, I realise that maybe she never wanted to be a mother. She isn't a bad mother. Not at all. But like most humans she never asked herself if she was ready to give birth, or even had the desire to start with.

I remember that afternoon like a scene from a film. The four of us and my father were at the table having breakfast on a Saturday. One of us, either I or Na'im, dropped some of the fried tomatoes we were eating on his shirt and spilt water on the table. Mother got angry and complained. My father had one of his outbursts and took all the water bottles from the fridge and spilt them on the floor. 'Why do you whine all day long? Just because a child spills water or stains himself? Now you can scream all you want to. Here you are! There is water everywhere now, so go ahead and yell . . . to hell with you!'

He put on his shoes and left. We were still at the table, staring at the food that had been laughing with us just a minute ago. My mother started mopping the floor. She cried so much I imagined that the spilt water was her own tears. I didn't lift a hand to wipe her tears, though. I just froze in my chair. Looking at her in her pain without uttering a word.

Today my mother cried again, but her tears were different. The tears of someone orphaned by hope. My grandmother, the Haifan, was gone. She had left time and my mother behind. My mother had no thorns. Her weakness and her hatred of life made her a rose without thorns. My grandmother was her thorns. She would always chastise my mother for neglecting herself and devoting her entire life to her children and husband. She always encouraged her to be independent. She would even urge her to leave the house for a few days and go to Jordan to visit her relatives.

When the border with Jordan was opened and she could go, my grandmother used to threaten my grandfather. If he mistreated her, she would leave him and stay in Amman. He, in turn, would ridicule her, saying she was free to go. But then he would soon thereafter come to our house, asking my mother to call her and ask her to return to Haifa as soon as possible. Sometimes he, too, went to Amman, but he used to get tired and complained that people there were garrulous. They ran chatter marathons, and would only shut up when they slept. Even then, some would keep talking. My mother laughed and told him they had twenty years of absence to make up for. They were afraid it would be the last time they saw each other. Their memories refused to erase the taste of separation, which had snatched so many years from them. He liked to sit for hours on his balcony, contemplating the street and the vast sea.

My grandfather started to yield to my mother's insistence that he should visit us more often and eat with us. He was silent and soft-spoken most of the time, except for that one day when he became the angriest I have ever seen him. Mother was trying to ease the burden of his silence and told him that God won't forget about him and would help them endure my grandmother's departure. I had never seen him scream that way at her or any of his children. He cried and his words were wet with sorrow.

'It's true he never forgets anyone. He fucked the Jews and they came and fucked us. And God knows who we're going to fuck over. Where was this God of yours when my mother died asking me to get her water? I put her down and went to get her some water and God took her life. Couldn't he wait a minute? Just wait for me to give her those few drops of water and then take her? No, he had to kill me. Since that day, I've never had a drink of water without remembering. May God humiliate them just as they humiliated us. And you tell me that he will help me endure your mother's death? May God not help himself!'

Mother didn't respond. She swallowed her tears, but she was shaking and whispered to God for forgiveness.

Grandfather fell silent. Those beautiful wrinkles on his face moved closer to one another, and like a rose, he withered. I understood then what it meant for my mother to be orphaned and grandfather to be widowed. It was as if Haifa itself had left him.

THE RUSSIAN COMPOUND

Her green eyes were persistent in their beauty and vitality. We exchanged smiles amid a controversial lecture by one of the 'new historians' about the modern Middle East. There was an uproar when he discussed the country's history, its myths about how their state was founded and the occupation of Palestine. I didn't understand why the lecturer's statements caused such controversy. He'd talked about the Palestinian and Israeli versions of events and insisted that the British archive compelled him, as an Israeli historian, to believe Palestinian narratives. Some of those present became furious. The lecture turned into one of those Knesset sessions where no one listens to anyone. There's just noise.

She was sitting one row ahead of me. We had exchanged smiles and a few sentences in previous lectures. I availed myself of the hubbub and tapped her shoulder. It was so silky-soft I feared I'd pierce it.

She turned round and smiled again. I leant forward and told her: 'Let's leave now before we both get headaches.' She hesitated a bit but then gathered her things. We spontaneously walked to the station and took a bus downtown.

We got off at the start of King George Street, where there was a row of falafel shops, but fifteen minutes after we'd eaten my stomach hurt. I preferred the falafel and shawarma in Haifa or from the Arab stalls in old Jerusalem; this was mediocre by comparison. She couldn't understand why I was berating the falafel of West Jerusalem; they weren't that different from those in Tel Aviv or Haifa, in her opinion. I felt sorry for her inability to distinguish good falafel from terrible. It's more than just a bad meal. Food is culture, and its pleasure no less fundamental than that of sex and love, and it is so much more. I explained that I thought they cheated, adding lots of baking powder to make their falafel puffy. It lacked spices and ground parsley. Teasingly, I told her I would insist she be stripped of citizenship because she couldn't tell good falafel from bad. She laughed and said she tried hard to be a good Israeli, giving her country what she could. I found it odd that she would describe the country as hers, when it had been less than a year since she emigrated from South Africa.

I suggested we go to al-Moskobiya, though as we were speaking in Hebrew I called it 'the Russian compound'. My tongue felt uneasy using only the Hebrew name. So I went on about the Arabic name, but without looking at her eyes or checking to see if she was even interested in listening to my little lecture. I repeated 'al-Moskobiya' several times. It was a name that had enchanted me from the first time I heard it. It was strange and I wanted to know more about it. I later learnt from a book that Russians were called 'al-Moskobiya'.

I couldn't see the connection but a friend suggested that it had to do with Moscow. To prove his point (he was studying linguistics) he said that in Russian 'Moscow' was said with a long 'ahh' that we Arabs don't use. Perhaps people tried to copy the Russian 'Moskva', tying all Russians to their capital. I adopted this narrative because it just about made sense to me, and gave meaning to a word I'd heard and liked.

We had reached Putin Bar when I looked for her eyes and saw her looking at me. I moved from expounding on linguistic matters to history and told her: 'The Petersburg-based Imperial Orthodox Palestine Society built this compound in 1861. It houses the Trinity Church and a hostel for the Russian pilgrims who started to come to Palestine in large numbers in the middle of the nineteenth century.'

I paused and saw two empty seats outside the bar. It was the beginning of the evening, and later these bars would be crowded. I got us two beers and we sat down. I looked at the quiet compound across the street as I leant back on the wall. Her green eyes radiated into mine, warding off the dazzle from lamp posts around the building and across the street.

I wasn't listening to her. She noticed that I seemed to be elsewhere and asked me if I was bored. I took her hand and felt it shake. I insisted on apologising. Kissing it and asking for her forgiveness, I told her that in speaking of this place's history I'd become lost in its most important detail: its present. Parts of it became a prison and a detention centre for Palestinians in this area. Thousands of people pass the building daily, as it's smack in the middle of the city near the municipal building, but I doubt they ever think of those detained inside or the torture they endure. I added that the prison is notorious for its torture methods. They strike detainees on their genitals.

She drew her legs in upon hearing that. I asked her what was wrong. She said she'd visited the museum the municipality had established there to commemorate Jewish groups that fought the British. The British were the first to use that part of the building as a detention centre. They executed Jews there, she said. I waited for her to mention the Palestinians who were also executed there by the British, but who don't exist in the museum or in her world. When she didn't, I asked her in a nervy voice, 'Why don't you mention the Palestinians, when they were the majority of those who were killed? Can't you see how history is falsified?' She shot back with a more daring look, but the mood became tense instead of tipsy. Sounding disgusted, she said:

'It's strange that you defend Arabs. They want to destroy us and throw us into the sea. Look at them. Their eyes are full of hatred and spite. I'm scared of them when they get on buses and even when I see them on campus. Their behaviour is strange. They chew loudly, put on cheap perfume and don't speak Hebrew properly. Can't you see their ugly eyes are full of hatred? I feel like they are ticking bombs that want to explode. I'm terrified when one stands in front or behind me in line. Why do you always want to defend them?'

I laughed when Nina was done and I don't know why. Actually I do. It was so absurd I could only laugh. Her opinions aren't surprising; in fact they are quite common. I've heard racist comments more times than I can count. But I was surprised that they were so solid and established when she'd only been in the country for less than a year. Nina, with her soft and stunning eyes, who told me about how ugly apartheid was in her country, and how happy she was that it was over. This same Nina who had yet to master Hebrew herself. Yet she feels free to trash Arabs and judge them without knowing a single one.

'I'm one of those Arabs you are talking about. Didn't you just say that my eyes were as wide as this fertile country? I laughed so hard because of your words. I am an Arab, Nina.'

She apologised and collected her things to leave. Why did I hide the fact that I was an Arab from her, she asked. I didn't answer and just shrugged. I remained calm and watched her cross the street and be devoured by the night. 'Why am I calm?' I asked myself. I stayed there and was gradually surrounded by other customers. One of them even took Nina's seat. I drank beer after beer, looking at al-Moskobiya Prison. I tried to listen for any voices that might sneak out seeking help.

When I stood up to head home, I felt hungry. I remembered that I had an orange in my bag. I took it out and started to peel it. I recalled that Israel had 'bought' the compound from Russia in the 1960s for $3.5 million, paid for with oranges it exported. It came to be known as the Orange Deal. 'So cheap! Three and a half million! Come and get it. Three and a half million's worth of oranges.'

Russia sells Israel this piece of land and the price is paid with oranges. Those who didn't own it selling to those who don't own it, so they can. It's a simple equation. I'd finished peeling the orange and was about to start eating when I remembered the story the museum guide had recounted so passionately, about Moshe Barazani and Meir Feinstein. They blew themselves up in their cells the day before the British were going to execute them. The explosives were smuggled to them inside oranges.

But the names of Palestinian resisters couldn't find a place in the museum.

Ghosts!

We are ghosts who only exist in our own imaginations. I looked at the orange and spoke to it:

'Things can't go on like this! Things can't go on like this!'

Tick tick tick tick tick tick

Is there another sound, please?

NEED

The dogs were mangling my body without spilling a drop of blood. The rabid creatures growled and followed me after I crossed the corner of the pothole-filled street. I ran, knowing full well I would be caught. Finally they pounced and started mangling my flesh. I was like a doll in their teeth. They chewed on me and not a single drop fell.

They can't get enough of my body, damn them. It was malleable, just like a doll's. And bloodless! I don't know how I could live without blood in my veins. I was sure there was blood in them. Blood as red as embers. Why do we use that expression? Embers aren't red. They're orange. The dogs chewed but couldn't tear me. They got angrier and more rabid, but I still shed no blood.

The sun struck fiercely at everything in its path. Heat found my body after the frosty cold of these autumn morning hours. Perhaps the heat found me because of the way the dogs were pulling me with their teeth.

It was on the corner of Salim al-Tawil's house (or Salim the Spy, as we called him) that the dogs jumped me. I don't know where they came from. No one appeared to help. I didn't scream. Why don't I? I felt intense pain, but it was a strange kind. As if my skin was so thick that the dogs grew tired of pointlessly chewing. Still they never gave up. They went on pulling on my thick skin while I lay down in pain and horror. I don't know which was more painful, the fear of the dogs attacking me, or their mangling of my body.

All the protests we took part in passed by Salim the Spy's house. I don't know whether he was a spy for sure, or if we just called him that because he worked with the police. He was strange, and the way he talked was even stranger. Like there was a magnet under his tongue pulling it down, so some letters seemed heavier than others. His blue eyes bulged even more when he yelled at us to move away from his house, as our chants grew loud and fierce.

Salim carried his belly with him and looked like a pregnant woman about to go into labour. I was sure that he was pregnant, but with hatred or anger, and would soon deliver; he never did. It was there, in front of his house, that the dogs started to mangle me.

The dogs were tired of my thick skin and my doll-like body. I was terrified of my own bloodlessness. I was terrified of the dogs' fury. I thought it was a nightmare, and it would end. When the dogs cast me away with the anger still seething in their teeth, I was relieved. Mangling my body was of no use. It was like rubber, flexible but lifeless.

They cast me away. I fell to the ground and lost consciousness. I came to when a policeman slapped me. It was painful, but he told me it was just a friendly slap. He wanted to make sure I was still alive. I was lying on the ground, and the neighbours had been concerned, so they'd complained to the police.

Salim the Spy was standing amid the police and pointing his index finger at me. He said I had mangled the dogs, and they had lost their teeth. I looked at my body. It had teeth marks. I had never intended to pull out the dogs' teeth, but the police were unconvinced, so they took me to the station.

One of the policemen asked me for my ID, but I didn't have one. I discovered that not carrying an ID card violated the law. Salim the Spy filed a complaint against me for breaking the dogs' teeth. His evidence was my bloodlessness. I tried to assure the policeman that I had cut my finger a week before and seen it bleed.

The policeman didn't like Salim the Spy, nor did he believe that I was a freak with no blood. He smiled and said that he would close the matter if I gave him my ID number. I just had to call my family to bring my ID, and he'd call it a day.

'I don't have an ID!'

'Why? Did you lose it?'

'No, I've never had one. I have no relation to IDs. I've never left the country so far and don't have a passport.'

'What is your ethnicity?'

'I live here and don't need an ID, nor do I need to prove my ethnicity. I'm simply here. I don't want to be anything. I'm me!'

'There is no such thing as "I don't want to be anything"! Are you Arab?'

'No, I have nothing to do with Arabs. I speak their language and have a weighty inheritance from their civilisation. I abandoned it, or it abandoned me . . . let's say we are divorced!'

'But you are an Israeli Arab and you live in this country.'

'You don't understand me. I have nothing to do with Israel. And there is no such thing as an "Israeli Arab". Stop this racist nonsense. Israel exists and I don't doubt that. It exists, as do I, but we have no relation. We share the same place. Actually, we don't share the same place. We each have our space and our illusion. I've never met Israel in my entire life. I don't like to meet anyone. I've cut ties with everyone I know. Because humans are an exhausting thing. Even those I don't know I cut off before meeting them. I have no desire to do anything except eat figs, and sometimes grapes too. I like the scent of jasmine, but if it's too strong I hate it. I enjoy looking at the moon, but when it disappears, I hate it and then yearn for it. My life is filled with minor concerns, as you see. I want the moon's silver threads to come down and caress my hair. I want them to realise my need for sleepiness and boredom, and my need for sleep. I don't want more. In fact, all I do is satisfy this need and exercise this right.'

'Are you Palestinian?'

'God forbid, man! I'm just a human who was mangled by dogs and left on the ground like a dog, because they couldn't find any blood in my veins. But I swear the dogs are wrong. I think they are old, and their teeth were about to fall out. That's why they couldn't eat my flesh and no blood was spilt.'

'But I saw them mangling the flesh of another passer-by. They tore him to pieces.'

'Really? Man! I don't know what happened to them then, but . . .'

'Who are you, then?'

'I am Nada. Believe me! My name is Nada.'

'Nada is a woman's name. You are a man.'

'It is my name. I chose it instead of the one my parents gave me. I love it. It's my name, I know it is. I am Nada by chance. Nada. No more and no less. And I only want to be Nada. I don't want to change my name. Nada is mine and I have got used to it. Can my name and I go now?'

'Just like that? Without an ID?'

'I told you, I never got an ID. I don't recognise the state or its papers. Can I leave?'

'Just like that? Without an ID?'

'Yes. I need some sleep.'

THIS BOOK WAS MADE POSSIBLE THANKS TO THE SUPPORT OF

Aaron McEnery
Aaron Schneider
Abigail Isaac
Abigail Walton
Ada Wilde
Adam Lenson
Adris Lorenzato
Afon Gold
Aija Kanbergs
Ajay Sharma
Alasdair Cross
Albert Puente
Aleksi Rennes
Alex Fleming
Alex Johnstone
Alex Krizan
Alex Liebman
Alexa Johnson
Alexandra Longhouse
Alexandra Stewart
Alexandra Tammaro
Alfred Tobler
Ali Colthurst
Ali Ersahin
Ali Riley
Ali Smith
Ali Usman
Alice Carrick-Smith
Alice Dewdney
Alison Lock
Allan Tennant
Alyssa Rinaldi
Amado Floresca
Amaia Gabantxo
Amanda Foulkes
Amanda
Amber Casiot
Amelia Dowe
Amitav Hajra
Amos Hintermann
Amy and Jamie
Amy Gitnick
Amy Lloyd
Amy Raphael
Amy Sousa
Amy Tabb
Amy Tighe
Ana Novak
Ananda Lima
Anastasia Sukhanov
Andrea Barlien
Andrea Larsen
Andrea Lucard
Andrea Oyarzabal Koppes
Andrea Timperley
Andreas Zbinden
Andrew Keddie
Andrew Kerr-Jarrett
Andrew Marston
Andrew Martino
Andrew McCallum
Andrew Milam
Andrew Place
Andrew Wright
Andy Marshall
Angela Erickson
Anita Trimbur
Anna Boorstin
Anna Finneran
Anna French
Anna Kornilova
Anna Milsom
Anna Zaranko
Anne Edyvean
Anne Frost
Anne Germanacos
Anne Ryden
Anne Willborn
Anne-Marie Renshaw
Annie McDermott
Anonymous
Anthea Parker
Anthony Fortenberry
Anthony Quinn
April Woodward
Archie Davies
Archontis Politis
Armin Nixdorf
Aron Trauring
Asako Serizawa
Asma Nizami
Audrey Holmes
Audrey Small
Barb Turk
Barbara Mellor
Barry John Fletcher
Beatriz Brown
Becky Matthewson
Ben Dutton
Ben Peterson
Ben Plouviez
Ben Thornton
Ben Walter
Benjamin Heanue
Benjamin Oliver
Benjamin Pester
Bern Bruty Mort Sal
Beth Heim de Bera
Bethan Lloyd Worthington
Bethany Everett
Bige Orer
Bill Fletcher

Billy-Ray Belcourt
Björn Dade
Brandon Clar
Brandon Invergo
Brekan Blakeslee
Brett Parker
Briallen Hopper
Brian Anderson
Brian Callaghan
Brian Isabelle
Brian Smith
Bridget Ingle
Brittany Redgate
Brooks Williams
Buck Johnston
Burkhard Fehsenfeld
Buzz Poole
Caitlin Halpern
Caleb Bedford
Callie Steven
Cameron Adams
Cameron Baillie
Cameron Johnson
Camp Bosworth
Carmen Smith
Carol Murashige
Carole Parkhouse
Carolina Pineiro
Caroline Lodge
Caroline Montanari
Caroline Musgrove
Caroline West
Caroline Sheriff
Catharine Braithwaite
Catherine Parker
Catherine Tandy
Cathryn Siegal-Bergman
Cathy Murray
Cecilia Uribe
Celia Kitchell
Cerileigh Guichelaar
Charles Fernyhough
Charles Heiner
Charles Rowe
Charlie Small
Charlotte Coulthard
Charlotte Ryland
Charlotte Whittle
Chelsey Blankenship
China Miéville
Chloe Horie
Chloe Wieland
Chris Clamp
Chris Johnstone
Chris Potts
Chris Stevenson
Christine Nestor
Christopher Fox
Christopher Lin
Christopher Scott
Christopher Stout
Clare Burgess
Clare Wilkins
Claudia Mazzoncini
Cliona Quigley
Colin Denyer
Colin Heinink
Colin Matthews
Colin Patterson
Collin Brooke
Cormac O'Callaghan
Courtney Lilly
Craig Kennedy
Cynthia De La Torre
Cyrus Massoudi
Daina Chiu
Daisy Savage
Dale Wisely
Dalia Cavazos
Daniel Cossai
Daniel Hahn
Daniel Sanford
Daniel Syrovy
Daniela Steierberg
Darren Gillen
Darryl Peers
Darryll Rogers
Dave Lander
Dave Appleby
David Anderson
David Binns
David Eales
David Gould
David Greenlaw
David Gylfe
David Hebblethwaite
David Higgins
David Morris
David Shriver
David Smith
David Wacks
Deborah Gardner
Debra Manskey
Delaina Haslam
Delilah Jaworski
Denis Larose
Derek Golden
Devon Lane
Diane Hamilton
Dillan Stenson
Dinesh Prasad
Domenica Devine
Dominic Nolan
Dominic Bailey
Dominick Santa Cattarina
Dominique Brady
Dominique Brocard
Dominique Hudson
Duncan Clubb
Dyanne Prinsen
Ed Smith
Ekaterina Beliakova
Eleanor Maier
Eleanor Weitzer
Elif Kolcuoglu

Elina Tripoliti
Elina Zicmane
Elizabeth Atkinson
Elizabeth Balmain
Elizabeth Braswell
Elizabeth Moor
Elizabeth Seals
Elizabeth Sieminski
Ella Sabiduria
Ellen Agnew
Ellen Beardsworth
Ellen Best
Ellie Goddard
Emily Drabinski
Emma Coley
Emma Louise Grove
Emma-Jane Lacey
Erika Westerlund
Erika Mäkipere
Erin Cameron Allen
Evelyn Reis
Ewan Tant
Fawzia Kane
Fay Barrett
Faye Williams
Fe Sasson
Felicity Le Quesne
Finbarr Farragher
Fiona O'Dell
Fiona Wilson
Fran Sanderson
Frances Evangelista
Frances Gillon
Frances Harvey
Frances Leach
Frank Rodrigues
Frank van Orsouw
Friso De Graaf
Gabby Bates
Gabriel Garcia
Gabriella Roncone
Garth Greenwell
Gawain Espley
Gawain Maroroa Jones
Gemma D'Alessandro
Gemma Hopkins
Gemma Rocyn Jones
Geoff Stewart
Geoffrey Urland
George McCaig
George Wilkinson
Georgia Panteli
Geraldine Brodie
Gerhard Maier
Gerry Craddock
Gilles Madan
Gillian Grant
Giorgi Gvaradze
Giuliana Cunningham
Glenn Russell
Gordon Cameron
Göze Saner
Grace Watkinson
Graham Blenkinsop
Grant Ray-Howett
Hadil Balzan
Hannah Levinson
Hannah Murray
Hannah Jane Lownsbrough
Hans Lazda
Harriet Stiles
Hazel Kight Witham
Heather Jeronimo
Heather Risher
Heidi James
Helen Alexander
Helen Berry
Helen Mort
Henrike Laehnemann
Howard Fischer
Hyoung-Won Park
Ian Betteridge
Ian McMillan
Ian Mond
Ian Randall
Ian Whiteley
Ilana Lifshitz
Inbar Haramati
Ines Alfano
Irene Mansfield
Irina Tzanova
Irwin Gaines
Isabella Gupta
Isabelle Cole
Isis Hockenos
Jack Brown
Jack Windle
Jackie Kearney
Jacob Goldberg
Jacqueline Haskell
Jacqueline Vint
James Attlee
James Avery
James Beck
James Cubbon
James Leonard
James Portlock
Jamie Risner
Jan Hicks
Jane Dolman
Jane Laurie
Jane Roberts
Janet Poveda
Janis Carpenter
Janita Sharon Jefferson
Jason Montano
Jason Timermanis
Jason Whalley
Jean Dubail
Jeff Worsham
Jeffery Huang
Jen Calleja
Jen Hardwicke
Jennifer Fain
Jennifer Gordon

Jennifer Harvey
Jennifer Lynch
Jennifer Rothschild
Jennifer Sarha
Jennifer Yanoschak
Jenny Huth
Jeremy Sabol
Jeremy Koenig
Jeremy O' Sullivan
Jess Hannar
Jess Wood
Jessica Harkins
Jessica Kibler
Jessica Queree
Jessica Webster
Jessie Lethaby
Jethro Soutar
Jo Armitage
Jo Lateu
Jo Thompson
Joachim Magens
Joanna Luloff
Joanna Trachtenberg
Joanne Tan Done
Joe Aguilar
Joe Segal
Johanna Rademacher
Johannah May Black
Johannes Menzel
John Berube
John Conway
John Gent
John Hodgson
John Kolaga
John Miller
John Purser
John Reid
John Shaw
John Steigerwald
John Whiteside
John Winkelman
John Wyatt
John Selby
Jon McGregor
Jonah Benton
Jonathan Blaney
Jonathan Busser
Jonathan Jefferson
Jonny Kiehlmann
Joseph Thomas
Joshua Cooper
Joshua Davis
Joy Paul
JP Anderson
Judith Gruet-Kaye
Julia Rochester
Julia Sutton-Mattocks
Júlia Révay
Julie Atherton
Julie Greenwalt
Julieanne Harmatz
Juliet Swann
Juliet Willsher
Junius Hoffman
Jupiter Jones
Juraj Janik
Justine Sherwood
Kaarina Hollo
Kaktus Leach
Kalina Rose
Karen Firmin
Karen Gilbert
Karen Mahinski
Kari Rodgers
Karina Brookes
Karina Cicero
Katarzyna Bartoszynska
Kate Beswick
Katharine Haake
Katharine Robbins
Katherine Sotejeff-Wilson
Katherine Spalding
Kathryn Drabinski
Kathryn Edwards
Kathryn Williams
Katie Freeman
Katie Zegar
Kay Caldwell
Keir Chetham
Keith Walker
Kelly Hydrick
Kenneth Blythe
Keno Jüchems
Kent McKernan
Kerri Boland
Kieran Rollin
Kieron James
Kirsten Benites
KL Ee
Kris Ann Trimis
Kris Fernandez-Everett
Kristen Tracey
Kristin Djuve
Kristin Glenn
Krystine Phelps
Kyle Pienaar
Lana Selby
Laura Jakobsson
Laura Pazour
Laura Wang
Laura Zlatos
Lauren Latulip
Lauren Stenning
Lauren Trestler
Laurence Laluyaux
Leah Binns
Leda Brittenham
Leila Billing
Leon Korte
Leona Iosifidou
Liam Wright Higgins
Liam Buell
Liliana Lobato
Lilie Weaver
Linda Jones

Linden Franz
Lisa Hess
Lisa McLeman
Liviu Tanase
Liz Clifford
Liz Ketch
Liz Wilding
Liz Rice
Lorna Bleach
Lorna Dielentheis
Louis Lewarne
Louise Ashon
Louise Evans
Louise Jolliffe
Louise Robinson
Lovisa Liljegren
Lucinda Smith
Lucy Hinnie
Lucy and Vanessa Marley Sutcliffe
Luiz Cesar Peres
Luke Gaillet
Luke Hayden
Luke Healey
Lydia Syson
Lyndia Thomas
Lynn Fung
Lynn Martin
Lynn Grant
Mack McKenna
Madalyn Marcus
Mairead Beeson
Mandy Wight
Marbellys Bayne-Azcarate
Maree Thomas
Margaret Jull Costa
Marian Zelman
Mariann Wang
Marie Cloutier
Marie Sandberg
Marina Castledine
Mario Sifuentez
Mark Lallemand
Mark Reynolds
Mark Sargent
Mark Sheets
Mark Sztyber
Mark Troop
Mark Waters
Marla Jackson
Marsha Lambrou
Marta Berto
Marta Figlerowicz
Marten van der Meulen
Martin Eric Rodgers
Martin Price
Martin Rathgeber
Mary Clarke
Mary Tinebinal
Mary Ann Dulcich
Matt Davies
Matthew Cooke
Matthew Coombe-Tennant
Matthew Crawford
Matthew Eatough
Matthew James Francis
Matthew Lowe
Matthew Miller
Matthias Rosenberg
Max Gordon
Max Spitz
Maxwell Mankoff
Meaghan Delahunt
Meeka Charles
Meg Lovelock
Meghan Ventura
Melynda Nuss
Merijn Douwes
Michael Aguilar
Michael Bichko
Michael Boog
Michael Franz
Michael Gavin
Michael Parsons
Michaela Anchan
Michelle Mirabella
Mike Abram
Mike Barrie
Miles Smith-Morris
Mim Lucy
Mo Tennant
Mohamed Tonsy
Molly Lincoln
Molly Tresadern
Mona Arshi
Monica Becerra
Morayma Jimenez
Morgan Lyons
Moriah Haefner
MP Boardman
Myla Lloyd
Myza Gouthro
Nancy Chen
Nancy Jacobson
Nancy Oakes
Naomi Morauf
Natalie Shpringman
Nathalia Robbins-Cherry
Nathan Weida
Neferti Tadiar
Negin Salmasi
Nick James
Nick Marshall
Nick Sidwell
Nick Slessor
Nick Twemlow
Nicky Reed
Nicola Mira
Nicola Protopapadakis
Nicolas Granger
Nicole Matteini
Niki Sammut
Nina Aron
Nina Lehman

Noel Weisenbacher
Norman Batchelor
Odilia Corneth
Olga Zilberbourg
Pamela Ritchie
Pankhuri Sahare
Patricia Schirmer
Patrick Hawley
Patrick Liptak
Paul Cray
Paul Ewing
Paul McGlone
Paul Milhofer
Paul Munday
Paul Myatt
Paul Nightingale
Paul Scott
Paul Segal
Paul Bangert
Pavlos Stavropoulos
Pearl Pandya
Pedro Ponce
Penelope Hewett Brown
Perry Ismangil
Pete Clough
Pete Keeley
Peter Humberstone
Peter Wells
Philip Herbert
Philip Warren
Philippa Jeacocke
Phillipa Clements
Phoebe Millerwhite
Phyllis Reeve
Piet Van Bockstal
Rachael de Moravia
Rachael Williams
Rachel Andrews
Rachel Baiman
Rachel Belt
Rachel Darnley-Smith
Rachel Rothe
Rachel Van Riel
Rahul Kanakia
Rajni Aldridge
Ralph Jacobowitz
Rebecca Caldwell
Rebecca Carter
Rebecca Jackson
Rebecca Marriott
Rebecca Milne
Rebecca Moss
Rebecca Peer
Rebecca Rushforth
Rebekah Lattin-Rawstrone
Renee Stroup
Renee Thomas
Rhea Pokorny
Richard Corley
Richard Ellis
Richard Hughes
Richard Mansell
Richard Smith
Richard Soundy
Richard Village
Ricka Kohnstamm
Riley Faulds
Risheeta Joshi
Rishi Dastidar
Rita Kaar
Rita Marrinson
Rita O'Brien
Rob Marshall
Robbe Van Petegem
Robbie Matlock
Robert Bresnan
Robert Gillett
Robert Hamilton
Robert Niles Weed
Robert Selcov
Robin McLean
Robin Taylor
Robin Whelan
Ronan O'Shea
Ronda Gomez-Quinones
Rory Williamson
Rosemary Horsewood
Rosie Ware
Roxie Ablett
Roz Simpson
RRT
Russell Backman
Russell Gascoigne
Ruth Curry
Ryan Bestford
Ryan Day
Ryan Pierce
Salena Copeland
Sam Ramsay
Samantha Byres
Samuel Gray
Sara Salsbury
Sarah Arkle
Sarah Bou
Sarah Brewster
Sarah Brown
Sarah Butler
Sarah Carr
Sarah Lucas
Sarah Shakespeare
Sasha Dugdale
Scott Adams
Scott Baxter
Scott Chiddister
Sean Johnston
Sean McGivern
Selina Guinness
Shannon Knapp
Sharon Levy
Sharon & Stephen Johnson
Shelly Albright
Shuchi Saraswat
Shyla Shrinath
Sian Hannah

Sienna Kang
Simak Ali
Simon James
Simon Robertson
Siriol Hugh-Jones
SK Grout
Stacy Rodgers
Stefano Mula
Stephan Eggum
Stephanie Miller
Stephanie Poletti
Stephanie Smee
Stephanie Wasek
Stephen Fuller
Stephen Yates
Steve Chapman
Steve Dearden
Steven Diggin
Steven Hess
Steven Norton
Stuart Allen
Stuart Cameron
Stuart Wilkinson
Suman Kumar
Summer Migliori Soto
Susan Dery
Susan Jaken
Susan Morgan
Susan Winter
Susan Wachowski
Suzanne Kirkham
Sylvie Zannier-Betts
Takamitsu Yamamoto
Tara Roman
Tatjana Soli
Tatyana Reshetnik
Ted Franco
Terry Bone
Theenu Satheeshkumar
Theresa Kelsay
Thomas Carroll
Thomas Counsell
Thomas Noone
Thomas van den Bout
Tiffany Lehr
Tim Hosgood
Timothy Baker
Toby Ryan
Tom Darby
Tom Gray
Tom Greig
Tom Stafford
Tom Whatmore
Tracy Northup
Trevor Brent
Trevor Wald
Tyler Giesen
Vandana Thirumale
Vanessa Heggie
Victor Meadowcroft
Victoria Huggins
Vijay Pattisapu
Wendy Langridge
Weronika Aleksander
William Mackenzie
William Wilson
Yana Ellis
Yoora Yi Tenen
Yort Jansen
Zachary Maricondia
Zahra Al Khudairi
Zoa Coudret